THE HOURGLASS

M.A.Robins

Order this book online at www.trafford.com/08-1189
or email orders@trafford.com

Most Trafford titles are also available at major online book retailers.

Cover Artwork: Don Fabricant

This is a work of fiction in the semblance of a memoir. Any similarity to persons, living or dead, though unavoidable, is coincidental. Aristotle thought poetry truer than history, and Coetzee relates how certain Africans say that only seven generations separate history from myth. Sometimes, this happens in a single generation; even a single year.

Note for Librarians: A cataloguing record for this book is available from Library and Archives Canada at www.collectionscanada.ca/amicus/index-e.html

Printed in Victoria, BC, Canada.

ISBN: 978-1-4251-8686-9

 www.trafford.com

North America & international
toll-free: 1 888 232 4444 (USA & Canada)
phone: 250 383 6864 ♦ fax: 250 383 6804 ♦ email: info@trafford.com

The United Kingdom & Europe
phone: +44 (0)1865 487 395 ♦ local rate: 0845 230 9601
facsimile: +44 (0)1865 481 507 ♦ email: info.uk@trafford.com

10 9 8 7 6 5 4 3 2 1

To
a Wild Irish Rose---
My loving wife Maureen

THANKS

And glad gratitude to Reina Attias,
for her indispensable determination and support;
and to Frank Aon for his early encouraging words.

Daedalus speaks to Theseus----

Ariadne's thread will be your link to the past.
Follow it back. Follow it back to yourself.
For nothing can begin with nothing, and it is
from your past, and from what you are at this
moment, that what you are going to be must
spring.

--Gide

It would not be enough for a poet to have
Memories, he must be able to forget them.

--Rilke

1

As THE BOAT BUZZES around Pelican Rock into the mouth of the little bay, Seferino throttles the outboard motor down to a whine; the hull settles low in the water and the boiling wake subsides to a simmer. Losing the lacerating air of speed he feels at once a damp red scorch on his wind- and sun-burned face, but ignores it in the slanting glide across the bay to the village side, straining through hot, watering eyes to spot his house, partly concealed by rampant jungle.

Mountains rise on two sides, one steeply, and a placid river comes down between, widening out to form a sprawling estuary with half a mile of beach thrust up in its *boca*. In the dry season the beach builds up and chokes off the river, leaving a shallow lagoon stalled behind it. Large palm-thatched *ramadas* ranged across the beach are restaurants, empty at this hour, and there are numerous similar *palapa* houses nestled in the steeper hillside where the people, native and foreign, live. It is quite late in a stilled tropical afternoon, and once inside the bay the sun is swallowed behind the village and he can see only on the highest hills opposite the last sunlight glinting from hundreds of coconut-oil palms, whose fronds thatch these roofs.

The water is calm enough for the boat, a fiberglass *panga* built
for speed and versatility, to land on the tiny beach in front of his
house, a beach that had been cleared when Epiphanio broke up
and lugged off the rocks settled there to make a retaining wall
for the hut he later built on one side. Only a few large, sunken
boulders remain in the way, so the boatmen must measure the
swells and the tide skillfully to ease between them onto the sand,
while the passengers time their jump from the bow, shoes in
hand.

It feels like a homecoming to him, though he has no home.
This is a place he comes back to with the excited anticipation of
a child, but he knows at the same time that he resides nowhere,
itinerant everywhere. Sauntering through his days as he can, *sans
terre,* and borrowing no time. And why should he not be glad here
to have it and yet not have it? He no longer has a phone number,
nor bank account, and without street address he gets his mail at
General Delivery. It is a persona he upholds without apology or
irony, like a perquisite of liberty won from penury unafraid. In
the village, shortage of cash is not poverty: tropical abundance
and the ocean's bounty sees to that. In this place it seems that
even the sky can afford the profligacy of its own stagecraft, equal
to the earthly.

Slinging his bag over his shoulder, he jumps to the beach and
retrieves from his pocket the pesos for the trip. Dashing forward,
Seferino grabs them with a shout of farewell, and, just before the
next wave slides in, reverses the outboard and speeds away around
the point. He watches him go, feeling the wet sink of sand in his
toes and the slough of seawater from his feet, then hunches up
the path for a few yards before putting on his sandals, and climbs
the stone steps to the back gate of the house and goes in, traipsing
through the dried-out garden twenty yards to the doorway, from
which the door itself was long ago discarded. Nor are there
windows to open or close.

To anyone else arriving the house might seem to be in ruins.
Over the weeks or months he is gone the jungle rushes in to

reclaim the house as its own: tendrils climb the walls. Blown leaves and the detritus from the palm roof covers the floors and the counters, covers the table and chairs, the bed hanging by four ropes from the *vigas*. Sometimes some of the village's roaming pigs break through a fence and make a mess of things in their forage; a stray chicken looking for bugs leaves droppings on the floor. But to him it is all there---the hammock and the carved mirror, the dishes and pots and pans, the pillows and bedding, bundles of moldy books. It will need only an hour or two of sweeping and straightening, checking to see if there is water in the tank and propane for the stove, look for and kill any scorpions that may have settled under the towels, and see to the kerosene lamps for lighting soon; the bedding grabbed up and shaken out, then thrown back on the hanging bamboo bed.

He has slipped into the village unseen, and is in the house. Perhaps a few gringos with binoculars have spied his coming, but not to matter: watching boats coming and going is a natural occupation for the so many idle hours in their day. He works with broom and wet rag and finds no scorpion, and after getting the house in order, he walks the short distance into the village to buy provisions for this night and the morning to come. Fresh cooking oil, coffee, eggs and a few vegetables, perhaps a can of large Pacific sardines, since it is probably too late to find fresh fish. Sugar and salt are still in the house, and a few other dry staples. The shopkeepers, most with only a table of goods in front of their house, laugh to see and welcome him back. Margarito at the post office hands him two or three letters he'd been keeping. They are addressed with no numbers, and they contain no surprises. One is from a friend looking for him, and hoping to visit if he is there.

As he walks back twilight is deepening fast, and the fleshy white bells of a datura shrub huddled against a brick wall in the gully just before the house are beginning to open, sly in twitching sensuality. Ramon the mason hails him from his patio, and his wife, Juana, from her dark kitchen waves. Once inside, he drops the net bag of groceries on the table and goes to light the lamps.

It is much darker in the house than outside, as it sits under the embrace and shelter of a huge *parota* tree, nearly Biblical in its dense loft and compass, whose branches of pinnate leaves sway over the roof and garden, like wands blessing them with a touch of enchantment. Even when daytime, the sunlight, leaking from behind or above, flickers dappled and cool, assuaging weariness, inducing daydreams and contemplation.

Now for the first time he sets in the chair beside the table, and goes over like an inventory the trip of this day. A sense of deliciousness envelops him in his new watch through the vacant doorway, toward the beach and the quiescent bay. Having sacrificed to a friend a fine green Maya jade bead, shaped like a bamboo section, he has thrown the proceeds into an airline ticket and bought a week in his sometime paradise. He'd flown from California in the early morning and, changing planes in Guadalajara, got to the Pacific Coast town in the mid afternoon. From the airport right off he took a taxi through town to the end of the road, a thirty- minute ride, to the last bustling beach, hoping to get there before the departure of the water taxi to his village farther down the coast. It had just gone, so he relaxed in the single thatched restaurant and ordered a beer and a shrimp cocktail, which came quickly, laced with fiery serrano chiles, tomato and avocado. He recognized a few village pangas still anchored off the beach, so he knew he'd get a ride in one. It was not hard to suppress impatience in the delightful shade of the restaurant. The hot, bright afternoon outside turned the turquoise water transparent by the shore, and a dozen gulls bobbed over the shallows. Maybe an hour later, Seferino showed up, and, loading plastic *garrafons* of gasoline into his panga, called out to him, "Vamanos! Vamanos, hombre!"

The ride, less than an hour, had the accustomed exhilaration of speed and noise and the sea was not so rough to force a grasp of the gunwales; he watched the rocky shore skimming by, imagining every meter gone a task completed, and felt in his shoulders the last hut recede. *The end of the road*---where it turned inland from that beach; not even the local boys would bother to tread the stony trail that scraped on faintly to the distant village. Waves shattered on the rocks and pelicans flapped vigilant above them. Only a boat could bring those who cared into the village, as it had no cars; electricity and telephone were hardly more than rumors, though to some perhaps a hope. That moment when the boat rounded the big, jutting island rock at the entrance to the bay--- not seen till the last seconds, and favored perch of pelicans and cormorants--- always brought a shock of release and jubilation, a return not merely to the fold but to what seemed like a celebrating *source*.

Now, basking in the glow of the lamplight on the table and the one still flagging his face, he felt a stunning glee. He had food, he had cigarettes, he had books, a gentle bed to sleep on while the sea knocked on the rocks below, and did not think he lacked anything. Anything at all. Time not worth measuring beckoned before him, and he would not think of what its limits might be, or need to account for it. The limits had nothing to do with him here, now, and his body, regained of fresh strength, felt as commodious as it ever had. Not merely comfortable but giddy with a sentience that expanded out and beyond the transparent but discreet integument of the house---so essentially exposed in its world---to where the darkness evolving outside murmured with jungle and sea sounds; to where the distant hollers of boys or the laughs of girls---- even *ranchero* tunes from somewhere--- cheered him. As if the house itself had made a pact with its world to privilege him. Here, alone and not alone, he would watch and applaud the acquiescent goodbyes of Time while startled by the concordance or resemblance of the crowd of sensations to some soaring musical intensity----wasn't all this unrivalled?

It was a while before he went into the kitchen to make some food, steaming up the few vegetables and rice---still in a jar under the counter!---and brewing a cup of the strong coffee from the *finca* of Juan Cruz high up in the mountains. A shimmer was seeping into the bay from around the mountain behind the house.

Taking the coffee outside, he knew it was coming from the ripe
moon that would soon flash over the town, and it was beginning
to drop daubs of white spackling that sprang out of wave crests
across the bay, twirling at their tops like ice cream drawn from a
machine. The rippling light brightened as he watched. Satisfied
that his timing of the trip had been good, he scraped out the food
onto a plate and wolfed it down. Nothing kept him from being
ravenous or impolite. And as he ate, he saw the wash of white
expand on the bay and break up into restless flecks of brightness
now jumping in the waves like little explosions, and knew that
the moon had just sailed over the hills, full. He wanted to jam
it all in, all, the sounds and tastes, the feast of eyes and fingers,
and the flawless, humid air, which he worshipped with the skin
of his body.

   "Hello night", he said aloud, and turned to the book he had
brought. It was a Fowles, who wrote novels of mysterious people
in intricate plots developed with a rich and nearly rash regard
for words. *The Magus* was fascinating, and he followed the story
avidly enough, if none the wiser for it. The intrigue, the sub-
tropical setting, suited the gleaming night, and those few people
passing on the path below the house, chattering and laughing,
did not distract or trouble him. But he stopped often to join the
night, the moon. Cradling the book on the smooth leather of the
table, the lamplight was genial, while the moon, high enough
at last, was brilliantly reflected in the bay, dazzling enough to
read the book outside. Between the ripples of moonlight were
dark troughs made to seem even darker than on moonless nights
by an endlessly inventive chiaroscuro. A proud, blinding white
was the moon now; avatar of the chaste goddess of myth, but
certainly nothing like a "woman rising from her tomb", as in
Wilde's *Salome*. As if under a spell perfumed by night jasmine
and wild ginger, he saw figments of ghosts intractably whisking
in shadowy corners of the house, as if characters in a Fowles'
fiction. Were they only phantasms? Maybe. All the same, they
were real, inviting or daring him to recall other days here, and

he thought that around the table another time he was sure to remember some.

Of course he would: in the inflexible certainty of the present, perennial and brimming with everything as it is, there can hardly be enough of recollection. How else vanquish---reckon, not forget---memory?

2

IT MIGHT HAVE BEEN midnight when the scene outside roused him from absorption in *The Magus*. There, standing on their own ineluctable shadows, everything was fixed, held luminous in tints of purfled silver. Thrilled as a mirror crazed, the bay was gorged by the doubled moon. He listened to the chirps and rustlings of the jungle, and heard coming on the breeze from the lagoon a frangible chorus of frogs, sung in rubber tones of oboe and bassoon. Only by that breeze were shadows shifting. Familiar and mysterious sounds wafted low, and the night was too beguiling to stay with the paper words. He walked into the drooping garden and reveled in the chilling white that lay on it like a blanched carpet, then stepped into the dusk of the little hut next door, used as a laundry, where someone years ago had painted on the mud wall the hippy motto "Keep on keepin' on". Built years before him, these houses were still called Hippie Heights, beyond the village as they were and rented cheaply. How could this ever be topped, he thought, wanting to fend off the haste of smug satisfaction that yet overtook him. He went out the gate and down to the datura blooms in the gully nearby, pausing to take them in, struck with unrelenting inebriation in some way further rectifying the night. He passed through the village, dead but for a lamp burning low and silent in one threshold, as if a ward to danger. On he went, crossing the tiny creek where a brood of pigs grunted in the mud, up over the hill and then along the straight path that went to a vantage above the beach. He paused there over the last steep way down and saw a lone figure striding barefoot across the lucent sweep of shore toward the hotel---just a scatter of palm huts like his---where the lives of vacationers drowsed in the moon drenched darkness. He could hear soft waves plashing on sand, a sound as sweet as a child's kisses, and watched them fill the trailed footprints with beaming mirrors that blanked out in seconds. A chilled breeze came down the river, and he remembered those first days he'd spent in the bay, at that same hotel almost ten years before. They'd driven down from their northern city, he and his wife, and the last leg of their trip had been in a four motor prop plane to the large resort town, then without a highway. The next morning they boarded a tourist boat that made a daily trip, landing on the beach in front of the hotel in a big wooden *canoa* that had already made several runs from the launch. Trudging up the sand to a crude counter in the calm shade of palm thatchery, they were led down a path through stony tropical gardens to a small palapa---he thought he could see it in the moonlight now----with a netted double bed and a small bathroom, tiny patio facing the bay. Hot water would be provided from a small boiler fired with coconut husks, and there would be lights from a generator until 10 o'clock. As they looked around and at each other in amazement, he began at once to search out words that would not sound like clichés in their telling. In his raptness, he found none.....so that first day and especially that first night, had given him the long desired taste of life on a 'tropical island', and he had never gotten over it.

After lunch and a short rest, they dropped acid, planned for weeks, and made love as the drug came on in the naked afternoon of sun and sea and sand, while they heard nearby shouts of swimmers and revelers and the squawk of the mascot macaw, flipping in the fronds of the hotel. In the evening they sat with suppressed giggles at a long table of fifteen people for dinner, faking a conversation with a couple they learned was from their own city. Though it could hardly have been more peculiar, they would later become friends.

Back in their bungalow, after the electricity went off they lighted some candles brought for the ritual of coming down from the 'trip', and marveled awhile at the place and at their place in the exotic adventure. The candles in the open air were burning down fast so he blew them out and lay on the bed in the sparkling darkness of the drug, still searching for compelling words---with little success. None of the ones they had exchanged in their trip lingered in his mind with more than amusement. She seemed then asleep, but the sound of insects in the deep night began to preoccupy his mind, then to crowd out his consciousness. The sounds appeared to be gathering and grouping out of a simple racket with a troubling but astonishing truculence, and it soon seemed to him that all these buzzing and screeching bugs were weaving a conspiracy, one with an adroit symphonic, or even philosophic, structure. Whether in the nightmare of a "bad trip" or simple hallucination, or not, they captured with their cacophony the whole pulsing night, as if abducting the known world---but for what ransom? Though he was as much entranced as baffled, yet it seemed more trying than his ransacking for words had been, as the meaning seemed broadcast in the code of intrigants, and he could not grasp a way to decipher it. It felt like the frustration of not solving a simple chess problem: *white mates in two*—but how? Something was there, *clearly,* but it was way over his head. Abruptly he grew alarmed, petrified, and lay there rigid in paranoia, hardly daring to breathe, mortified to think she lay beside him not asleep but this quiet because she too was blanched with fear, terrorized. In suspense he waited for her to scream---minutes, hours?---but was at last delivered unknowing to a color-shot slumber. In the morning, bleary but serene, she told him she did not remember hearing anything strange.

The figure crossing the beach soon slipped into the shadows of the hotel and vanished. A thin flow of river found a channel through the sand to the bay, and it would not be hard to cross. But that tempted him less than the whim of continuing along the path up-river, which first went down by the rank sidewaters of the lagoon, where the frog chorus was now wobbling loudly, advancing into the jungle to a majestic stand of old coconut trees, their tops so inscrutably towering the moonlight was nearly unobstructed. He continued a further short distance as far as Benino's banana grove, where he hesitated for a time bemused as loony shadows cavorted beside the quivering stalks. An echo blew up over the whispers of wind: just beyond the scrub, the river purled among rocks of gneiss or granite. The perimeter around where he stood was diffused, and the world under the floodlight moon lay exposed skeletal, defined like the dream of a fantast. He knew it a marvel to be standing there, astounded alone in rich silence. Not a bird stirred; the frogs had ceased. No, nothing could top this, he exulted, be smug as you like! He wandered yet, until he felt his tired limbs giving out, so retraced his steps home to find the tangle of his bed and, wrapping himself in the gorgeous oblivion of the sheets, dropped at once into a justified and undreaming sleep, without disturbance until the cock-brazen dawn.

As he awakened he felt a dampness rising from the floor, and stayed huddled in the sheets. The bed lightly swayed with his movements, and as he waited for the light to come up he listened to fresh choirs of birds grow louder and more varied as they awoke. By the time he heard the contentious squabbles of a flock of moon parrots, sunlight was heating the dry hills on the opposite side of the bay---first to get the sun and last to lose it. The pelicans appeared at their stations on the rock at the far point. He swung his feet over and onto the cold floor, and checking for scorpions made his way to the kitchen to put the little Turkish coffee pot on the stove. He watched the grounds sink in and waited for it to foam up, then swirled it around a bit before pouring it through a strainer into a green pottery cup. Spooning in a little sugar he took it to the table, where *The Magus* was still face down with another hundred pages to read. He pushed it aside and lighted a Delicado, his cheap smoke of choice here, though he really preferred their taste. He liked that there were only eighteen in a pack, slender for a pocket, which had on the label a 19th Century bust of a lady in a chignon. He thought about standing dazed in the banana grove the night before, the wobbling frog voices, the powerful moonlight. But he was eager for the eggs he would make for breakfast, so, rinsing the pan from the night before, he sliced a couple of potatoes thinly and put them on to fry, wishing he'd soaked some beans overnight. He diced a chile, threw it in a bowl with two eggs and forked them smooth, waiting, lost in thought for some minutes, for the spuds to soften, before emptying the mixture into another frying pan.

While he sat at the table eating, he gazed through the doorway as the bay came alive with revving motors, and a dozen pangas shot around in their village business, ferrying passengers or heading out beyond the point for fishing, to feed their families and supply the restaurants on the tourist beach. The old wooden Lucinda chugged off, puffing diesel smoke, to the resort town with two stiff rows of passengers somnolent on the hard benches. It could take two hours. How many trips had he made on her? There had been many before the advent of pangas, slow and weary, and mostly too fume-filled to do anything but bide time, or watch the old rotund pilot scan the water ahead for hazards. He remembered returning on it from the 'hospital' with his wife and their five-day-old son just before one New Year's Eve years ago. They landed late in the short, near-solstice afternoon, and it seemed as if the whole village had come out to greet them and their new, wrapped bundle. He was still in the cast of a broken leg, hobbling with desperate effort on crutches up the path to their house, a different one at that time than now.

3

THE SPELL OF MEMORY was shattered when he heard someone shouting his name from the path below. It was a woman's voice, surprising in its lilting ring. He jumped up and leaned over the wall to see Becky, who lived in the house behind his, fifty yards up the hill. She came on through the back gate, in a muslin dress trimmed in ruching, laughing and idiotically waving both arms.

"I saw your light on last night and thought you were back, but didn't want to be bothering you", she said. A Belgian woman, she stayed in the village much of the year, but spent summers in Brussels or Paris doing chalk copies of Old Master paintings on the sidewalk. Paid like an organ grinder, she was proud but a little sad to leave her work behind for summer rains or pedestrian feet to erase. Her own art, which she worked on most days "in the good light", had some merit but not much originality, he thought. The skill of her copies amazed him however, a few of which---on paper---she had shown him. Was her talent spent out in simulations?

"Hey, come on in, want some coffee?" he shouted.

"But no, thanks anyway, I just had mine", she said, and came bouncing through the doorway and sat down at the table. Not too pretty a girl, he thought, with her long face and slightly yawing expression, but with so lithe and lively a figure, and flaxen hair, he was stirred and wanted her right away.

"How are you----been here the whole time since I left?" he asked.

"Ooh, yah, but I went off to Guad to get some better art supplies", she said in her Flemish inflected voice. " I went with Margo, so we spent a few days with her family on the lake, in Chapala. Lots of good whitefish, and bunches of kids. It was fun, but the noise you know, it got on my nerves. I came back a little early, by myself. I've been working well, trying to keep at working...working----I don't know what else", she threw out at the end, in the hoarse meter of resignation.

"How've things been here?" he questioned, with some curiosity, but mostly to keep the mood open. She could turn suddenly morose far more easily than he could.

"Ooh, well...well...trouble always with the water, Antonia sends her *mozo* down at night to turn off my tank, so I have to check it all the time. Do you have water?" she asked with a furtive glance.

"There's been enough so far, but I haven't used much yet", he replied, thinking of the shower, and the salt he had yet to wash off. Their water came from above the waterfall behind the village, which several different lead pipe systems brought directly into the houses. The farther along the pipe a house was, the stingier the trickle; many houses had installed a holding tank. Hers was next down the pipe from his, and Antonia's down from hers. In the dry time of year this made for a strained hierarchy of water!

She jumped up and scurried to the bathroom to turn on the shower, as if the sink wouldn't do. " Lots of water", she said, and he could hear as well. "I let your tank get full, and then turn it off", she added. Seeing her flounce around the house was very inviting in the fresh morning, and he let her fine female energy take him over. "Did you find everything alright?" she blew at him, now actually dancing around, "there was a couple staying here for a week or two last month... Martita put them here...maybe she has some money for you", she added in a confiding whisper. "I think they were friends from San Francisco. They looked scared the whole time, and asked me on the trail one day what to do if they got bitten by a scorpion". She showed him a grimace, since they both knew that scorpions sting, not bite. Then she twirled over to him and ran her hand through his hair, tap-dancing in place, and asked how long he was staying.

"A week or so" he answered, resentful of having to measure time even by mention of practical limits. He was here to be out of time. "But I'll be back in the summer with Nico," he went on, giving her a look meant to settle her back down in the chair. As if reading his mind, she sat down, crossed her legs and lighted one of his Delicados. She puffed in silence for a while, twitching the free foot, and said she was going to the beach later to sketch Mariana, the boatman Jorge's wife. But she wanted to have some fish for lunch too, would he like to come along? She hadn't been to the beach for a week, and thought it was time for an outing, time to hang out a little. Before he could say a word, she sat straight up and grabbed his arm, entreating him to come, with eyes the vivid blue of delftware, then abruptly lurched back in the chair and said he should do whatever he wanted. It was startling to watch her face color in storm, the few freckles seeming to fade out, and he leaned over toward her earnestly. "Becky, sure, I'd love to go to the beach with you, I was planning on going down, I'll be ready in an hour...let's meet at Domingo's", he spat out, as she jumped up into another little dance to the hanging bed where, sitting down and giving a spry push, she murmured coyly that Jorge had some good pot for her, it was for the sketch she was doing, and they could smoke it later. She smiled at him and shook herself before jumping up. Pausing in the doorway she said "Yah, good, let's just meet on the beach in an hour or two, but at Steve's not

Domingo's---I don't like the *cabron* who works there", the last growled as she flew down the steps.

He could hear her singing up the path to her house, and her energy marshaled his as he slouched in the chair. He felt excited but also dismayed as he realized how she might appropriate his time here. But he would let her---certainly not oppose it---for tonight the moon would still be full and time be full, the only limit one imposed on it. But the unbidden image of an hourglass flashed in his mind, top-heavy with sand---emblem of the inevitable, a caution that all beginnings foresee their ends. Meanwhile, forbid nothing and nothing shall be forbidden you. Those who question with wrinkles on their foreheads deserve the headaches they get. If such thoughts did not completely assuage his doubts, it was because there were certain places in his heart, like shallows in a lake, past which he was afraid to swim. But he did swim out past them---didn't he?---out to the deeper lake where he felt his limbs freed and supple, but the return to shore led back through those same shallows, a victory incomplete; for only so long could you stay in the deep. As he mused, a yacht not far off his beach maneuvered for an anchorage and he shrugged off these doubts, relishing the time that would gracefully be *his* time, in the rhythm of its own ripening and in the similar rhythm of surrounding life---coeval in their comprising by grateful embrace.

4

THROWING THE DISHES IN the sink, he ran water on them, then rinsed out the coffee pot and decided to have one more shot. Again he watched the foam come up once or twice, loving the plain ritual of it, and took the cup into the garden. In the dry cycle, it was as sadly reduced as the browning hills around, and probably hadn't been watered, though there were still a fair number of thriving plants--- jasmine and ginger, big elephant ears fluttering along the stick fencing near the front gate; on the back slope, the color of the bougainvillea draped faulty. Not much good soil here, built on the rocky slope above the shore, he thought---for the hundredth time. And undiscouraged creeper, struggling in flaccid clumps. His wife---now ex-wife---with patience and determination had planted much of it in her years, and he felt a nagging duty to keep it up as well as he could. Of course, in the rains, in the summer, when he came with his son for six or eight weeks, it was easy. Now he thought he'd better give it a drink, and found the hose still connected to the sink in the tiny laundry hut, and began to shoot, with thumb for nozzle, sprays around the dry ground. The sound of it splashing on the elephant ears was pleasing enough, but there was also a sense of doing *good*; why should this nag at him, not pleasingly?

A woman flounced through the gate, and he lowered the hose, thinking, Why are these women always flouncing? But then, weren't we all flouncing, slightly delirious from escaping the harsh North, from being suffused with the sensuous air of the tropics? Or was it just in the accommodation to walking on the rough paths of the village? Martita swept in, silver jewelry clanging on the path, in a step that was rather more like a pounce. Her feet were shod in ixtle fiber sandals handmade by an obscure tribe in the mountains of Oaxaca, while her blouse was sheer cotton, embroidered with fantastic animals and woven on a backstrap loom somewhere down in Chiapas---- these no doubt provided by Maggie, the expat doyenne of the village. Without a bra, only the embroideries teasingly covered her breasts, though it was not clear she wished them to be hidden.

"I watered the garden *veddy* few days ago", she said in a high English accent, haughty in her chic, "while my friends were staying here". She went on to explain that they were going to stay with her at first, but she thought since his house was empty it would be "jolly to give them their own space"---*and keep hers undisturbed,* he knew she failed to add. "They paid rent money, of course, but I had to use it to buy a new tank of gas when they left", she announced, and hoped he found the house in *dear* shape. "It was alright", he assured her, ignoring the sticky accounting. As she shuffled before him he was unable to forget that a few years ago he'd gone with Martita's boyfriend Joe, on a trip to Huichol country in Nayarit. Joe, a teacher at a state college in California, had gotten some sort of grant to do a thesis in anthropology, and chose as subject the Huichols---he supposed---because they were not far away, and because they were religious about *peyote*. The Don Juan books were a rage, so it seemed obvious that Joe wanted to produce his own contribution to the New Age, under a similar academic guise. But at the end of his own week-long leg of the trip---planned for plain adventure---an incident occurred that would strain their relations severely: on the windy, desolate airstrip where he climbed into the single engine job, flown by a priest-pilot, returning to Tepic---while Joe stayed behind to continue 'research'---Joe had told him to tell Martita that he loved her. Failing to deliver the message, Joe charged, had caused Martita to sail off on a yacht with another man. But he did not remember seeing her --they were then living in a house the other side of the village---and she certainly had not come by to see him; maybe gone by then, for all he knew. But hadn't Joe always bragged about their 'open' relationship? No matter, Martita's affair was his fault.

He crimped the hose as she stood outbidding the garden, eyeing him with the openly challenging expression of a woman who would not be fazed. "How are Donna and the boy", she asked. "They're doing well", he replied, "though I haven't seen them for a month, I've been in California". Was it a real concern for how they were, or just a probe to see what fodder for gossip he might cast out? And somehow the query turned his composure qualmish, as when the sun is blotted by a sudden, unwanted cloudburst. Joe had written his account of the trip in which he, the crass companion, had been portrayed as a fool. Most of the book told a narrative of the magical doings at the *rancho* of a Huichol shaman; Joe's return to the mundane was described with an oily smirk, and delivered in tones of creaking profundity. Of course Martita came back from her cruise of romance...and was rather smirking at him now; but only for a pregnant moment until, prancing to the gate, she tossed her thick chestnut hair to the wind and called back to him, "You should come round to my house"----the same Epiphanio had built years before-----"and see all the Huichol things *I* have." For sale, he guessed. "Yeah, sure I will, I'd love to see them", he let out of his mouth, and instantly regretted. He realized that, before he could say anything about the strangers put up in his house, she had cancelled him, channeling a behavior not of his choosing, into a mood he disdained---but why blame her? Grasping the thwarted hose in his hand, innocuously shy of its business, it was as if his cock had gone down before the final jolt, and he stood there just like the fool Joe had portrayed. And he was a fool, wasn't he? Only a fool could be so mute and undefended---or *over* defended. Dropping the hose to spurt as if redeemed, he went into the laundry hut and turned off the faucet. He stood there, trying to regain purchase on his center, and stared through the space under the hanging fringe of palm roof to the undulating waters of the bay, and began to smile, forced a smile, until he could not hold back a surge of chuckles that became a laughter so sardonic it bent him over into a mock burlesque. *Graceful ripening time*, is it? He did his own little dance there, chiding himself for being, yes, a fool!--- knowing that his qualm was for the mask that so poorly hid his unquieted jealousy. What the right hand gives let the left receive, 'till death do us part. And when the left receives nothing from the right, when death parts them from us? And when there's no me to know that I am not here, who will rejoice? Maybe a crowd, that's who! *Gaudeamus igitur*, you bet! Chortling with abandon, he floated sprightly into the house to make ready for his jaunt to the beach.

5

GLIDING PAST THE TABLE, he eased into the hammock for respite and felt the house shudder as if from a *temblor*. A large *matrimonio*, it was hung from the vigas at an awkward angle, and the wooden sounds he heard were disquieting. He remembered the time he'd collapsed in one, so, bracing himself hopefully safe with feet still on the floor, he made himself test it before surrender, bouncing lightly up and down until persuaded it was secure. It was a marvelous piece of craft from Yucatan, and stretched out made a blue and white symmetry of pure cotton strings. As he lay back and studied the weave of the palm fronds above, he recalled watching them go up when the old roof could no longer be patched. Twenty men from the village, off duty boatmen or waiters, grocers, young slackers, pressed into service to create the interlocking of the fronds, all hands together tamping each down tight before tying them to the wood frame with jungle vines. He'd insisted on vines because they withstood moisture better than rope, so lasted longer. They were also more authentic, looked better. Curious how gringos wanted to live in authentic native palapas, while natives wanted to live in modern cement block bunkers, which they built as soon as they had the money---money earned from making palapas for the gringos!

Now swinging peacefully, concentrated on the roof, he was at the same time still stewing from Martita's visit....When he'd read Joe's typescript he realized how a desire, or *need*, for pith and wit made tricking out a story--- "history"--- inescapable, even as you believed you were faithfully recording it. Conrad had called this *the essential sincerity of falsehood,* in *Lord Jim,* swaying the convention that *lurks in all truth.* Still, he knew his own account might be no less gussied.... And was Joe here too? Were they still together? Did it matter? Their turbulent connection provided gossip to the small expat colony, and gossip, like boat watching, was a serious occupation---one possibly necessary for the not completely vain hope that attention to the small might obviate the need for attention to the large. Sometimes visitors would ask, *What do you do here?* in a tone more incredulous than curious, and he would say he did the same things they did, but with less equipment. Often this brought an embarrassed silence, which he would do nothing to break.

He got up to light the burner on the tank for a shower, emptied some dry beans from a jar into a pan of water, paced around eating a banana, then unpacked the duffel bag, laying out his clothes and sundries on the bed. Swimsuit and shirt, net bag for towel and pesos, ancient bead necklace to complete the look. Testing the temperature, he took off his gym shorts and stepped under a thin, tepid spray; the tiny room had a twisted wire window, and through it he could see several men and a woman on the yacht throw some things into a dinghy tethered alongside. By the time he finished showering, they were all in it, rowing off to the beach in town. He dried himself, threw on the clothes and, slinging the net bag from his shoulder, headed off to his rendezvous.

6

HE PAUSED AT THE gate, almost fondling it in admiration. He and Octavio had taken the good part of a morning putting it together with branches and leftover bamboo sections, framing it with some spare mesquite timbers.... *Want not, waste not---*that's how *he* wants it to go---so make do with whatever is lying around; a virtue in some places, but here, nigh a necessity. With only a machete and a practiced eye, Octavio worked it all up, having brought the only part that would not have been lying around: a spring. Even the catch was fashioned from a piece of rope found on the beach, which he snugged back over the smooth, whittled post as he left.

He went down the path into the gully, where the datura glimmered with its flowers closed and slunk morbidly, as though not sleeping but dead. It sat in front of the only red brick house in the village, built by an outsider years ago, whose patio was cluttered with potted plants, facing a tiny creek that would not run until the rains. Pipeline Jim he was called, having brought down the first water pipe to the houses in the village. Married to a much younger local girl, he had recently built a large cement house high up on a hill, whitewashed and looking like a castle, and had given this little cottage to some of her siblings.

The path to the village was worn as well as could be, and was trod in just the easiest sinuate way past the stones and boulders and protruding tree roots; not even a bicycle could manage it. He reached the village center and the hut of Eva, who sold beer and soft drinks, hauled up eternally from the beach landing by her husband Pedro. Lisping Eva who, once in a while, could be persuaded to fry up some eggs for a breakfast postponed by languor. She sat in the shade with a sly, permanent chuckle as he went by, while her two little girls in panties stumbled around the fly-blown *ramada* with the chickens and cats. When he walked by with his son, she always sang a teasing ditty, "Nicolas, Nicolas, Coca Cola nada mas." When Nico got old enough, he'd veer off another way to avoid passing her.

Without lingering he went through the village to a cement bridge over the shaded creek, lightly flowing, a river only in summer. The bridge had been the recent project of Umberto, perhaps as a kind of penance since he was a spiteful, violent drunk, and it was no longer necessary to hopscotch from rock to rock in the crossing. On the other side the path ascended the same hill of the night, at the top of which he looked back, down to the village and the beach at the mouth of the creek. The dinghy from the yacht was off to one side with no sign of the sailors. The path continued along the side of the hill with the bay receding below, past houses both foreign and native, and it was a peaceful amble after the stumbling climb. Strings of mules and horses went by toward the main beach, where the day tourists would rent them for a trip to the waterfall. Girls small or lanky went by, carrying trays of warm pies to be sold on the beach. This contained world---rather all its activity---was moving toward the beach glittering below in adamant morning light, and all of that going kept its own reasons. And his, of course, was to meet Becky down at Steve's, *el vago playero*, the restaurant of the Beachcomber. And it occurred to him that they were all like beachcombers, all set down on a sparkling beach in the middle of There, gazing around in rapt wonder, or simply bored or bemused, until the unmerciful sun beat them into submission. How could changing one beach for another seem like such a victory? Could it change There into Here?

He stood where he had the night before, overlooking the beach before the steep way down. A bird sang in a small tree nearby, solitary but steadfast, and he thought of a New Yorker cartoon he'd once seen, where a man walking in the woods passes a branch on which a small bird is perched, who says to him "I do not sing because I am happy, I am happy because I sing." *When you sing the blues you lose the blues,* a jazzman once said. And here was this bird, wiser than a pretending owl, whose solo was not a twittering or screeching like many of the jungle. In his mind he followed the songster as if past the shallows of the lake and into the deep water where his limbs were free, and he wanted to sing, and he believed he could sing. As he clambered this time down the steep path to the beach where he knew the sun was hammering and everyone was waiting for the first tourists to arrive, the birdsong lingered inside him, and it was surely not just the song of the beachcomber. But when he got down to the beach and took off his sandals and began the trudge over the scorched sand toward the restaurants, he was not so sure. Was it because the burning orb of sun had no trouble filling to the brim a sky even so vast as this? His limbs felt not so free as they struggled and sweated to carry his body through the huge, hot morning, but he foresaw the ease of palm thatch minutes ahead, and there the song could be reprised.

When he crossed the shallow channel of the river he escaped the burn and continued on striding the wet shore; a good breeze dried his sweat to a thin slippery sheen. He was cooled, and the weight came out of his legs and settled into the drag of sand under his feet. After the weariness and heat, a chill of freeness spread; as it took him by surprise, he desired it but couldn't make out where it would lead, and knew even less what it would ask of him there.

So with a lighter step he walked down the beach in the fluid shore, where last night's figure had left shining footprints, and in his shoulders he felt Maggie's binoculars watching him go from her aerie in the compound on the hill behind the beach. Maggie, who traded in Indian crafts from southern Mexico---what Martita wore---did not leave her house much, preferring to conduct there a kind of hip jungle salon. She watched the comings and goings in the bay and on the beach, and often knew who was doing what and sleeping with whom before anyone else. Since he would suspend or defer calculations---forfeiting them to chance and whim--- for at least the time spent here, he had not yet thought about a visit to her, but imagined it likely.

7

RIGHT AROUND THE MIDDLE of the beach, beyond the river's mouth and the dune that will wash out to sea in the next storm, the restaurants began. In front of each was a young hawker with menu in hand who would rush to entice the landing tourists into his own palapa. Domingo's was the first, and the swaggering beach boy who lounged in a reclining chair was the *cabron* that Becky disliked, and was probably afraid of. His good looks were as much a result of a style of bold confrontation as of his nearly pure Indian blood. Though past twenty, he had no wife in the village, preferring to pursue the gringas that washed ashore with the regularity of the tides. His tips were only survival cash, as the job was a convenient station from which to assess the fresh arrivals. He'd be alert for any woman of a certain age, preferably by herself, toting luggage.

"*Ola amigo, que onda?*" he called out, with an insinuating tone of conspiracy, "*sientete, por favor.* Where you going?" He sat down in the next chair of the row set up for the soon to be arriving hordes, and just laughed in reply. It was not conversation that Manuel wanted, just the banter of mock friendship, while he waited for the boats. It felt good in the chair, with the sun on his back, and he thought that if Becky was not yet at Steve's, he would see her coming. She might not like his sitting there, but he figured to recover more of his own initiative, rising to meet her from the disapproved place: a petty calculation.

"*Que pasa con tu y Becky?*" he asked. "I don' know, she don' like me", Manuel said, with a sneer. "I try to be friend, she no want friend. You my friend, *verdad?*" *Como no*, he said, we're friends…so how about a *cervesa?* Manuel shuffled in his chair and called up to the makeshift bar to bring a beer, and soon a fleet girl came running out with it. "*Gracias, mi hija*", he said, handing her 10 pesos and waving off any change. "Your *esposa?*" Manuel asked. "We split up" he answered, "and the boy is in school in the States", he added, to forestall any further talk of it. "You have girl friend, amigo?" Manuel pressed, and when he said yes, many, he had many, Manuel let out a guffaw of both approval and doubt. He was the Latin lover, not this old, gray gringo. And with that, Manuel jumped up, saying the boats would be in soon, it was time to get ready, and he dashed into the restaurant; it was pointless to guess what else he needed to prepare.

The beer had gone down fast, and he sat looking out on the little bay, now so tranquil and plainly ordinary, with its respectable swell of regular waves dropping down, the very image in a deceptive travel brochure. On the hillside nearest to him, sloping up behind the hotel, the coco palms tossed fretful in the breeze, glabrous in the sunshine, and gold splashed over the dustiest rock. The glare no longer seemed merciless at all, and the heat was not punishing as it had been, but benign and comforting. The *chill* of freeness!---*shiver* was better. What did he mean by it anyway? Was it merely a coy literary device to avoid the banal word "freedom"? Still posing, if only to himself. And suddenly, the memory of a sunset on a yacht off the coast of Baja flashed in his head, where he and the rest of the crew--- paying guests--- had sat with the skipper munching on crudités, no less, drinking good bourbon and Scotch, while belowdecks Sally the cook prepared another great dinner with the lobster and abalone they'd bartered fish hooks for that morning in their anchorage. Tired and exhilarated, after a day of fast sailing and whale watching in Magdalena Bay, bantering in the camaraderie of an ocean cruise on a fifty foot cutter, it had been a moment to convince even the most reluctant spirit how well everything was with the world. And this was the sensation he rejoiced in now, sitting before the placid bay, and waiting for flaxen Becky to waltz in view; a sensation that the world was fine, not as complicated as his own self-absorption trapped him sometimes to believe, and that there was more power in *relish* than in *doubt*. Under his feet he felt the warm sand and raised a footful, letting it sift out between his toes, then did the same with a handful, and thought of the hourglass. Against his forearms was the smooth wood of the chair, and a phrase of music turned in his head---Schumann or Schubert?---while his gaze followed one of the cuter pie girls walking by with a tray teetering on her shoulder. One of Juana's daughters, Juana who had waved to him the night before, and she carried *pie de limon*, made with key limes and piled with perfect meringue; the tray would be empty within the hour. All his perceptions were of relish.

Feeling the beginning of a burn on his thighs---perhaps half an hour had gone by in his reverie---he got up, hoping Becky was somehow at Steve's already, and walked up into the shade of the palapas ranked along the upper beach. Waving at Manuel, who was scolding the girl that brought the beer, a few steps took him into the next hut where he did not linger, and then into the much more capacious and finely groomed restaurant of Steve the Beachcomber. Steve was a foreigner who had come years ago, one of the legendary founders, from a career as a union agitator. His wife was a native, and they had several children, each named after some socialist hero. Steve was not an ideologue, but more like a character from Steinbeck, a solid family man whose passions included drinking moonshine tequila and playing chess. He and Steve had had many a session with both on late afternoons when the beach and the restaurant were deserted. His conversation was always lively with reminiscence and useful local information.

A few people sat at the tables, but he could not see Becky. Several couples at one---probably overnighters from the hotel--- were noisily drinking from flower-adorned coconuts, enjoying themselves with a conspicuous abandon. And, he noticed, in complete oblivion. Costumed in tennis gear, the men had shirts emblazoned with advertising, and the women shrieked under comic sombreros, one sporting a plastic iguana tied on its crown, bought no doubt on yesterday's beach. All had white sneakers on their feet, cumbersome in the sand, and were wildly disputing each other's version of some fishing excursion of a previous day. They barely glanced at him as he walked by looking for Becky. He wandered to the back of the palapa, past the kitchen, to find the bathroom. It was not much more than a porcelain pot concealed by some upright palm fronds, near which a few tethered pigs grunted, efficiently carrying out their task of garbage disposal until the time when they would themselves appear on the menu. When he emerged, he looked past the refuse and detritus up the river, a far level sweep until it narrowed and disappeared into the defile of high sierra. Trails went up on both sides to pass a thinning scatter of palapas, but only the trail on the right bank went up for miles to a large town in the interior. He had never been more than two or three miles up the river, where there was a rapids that narrowed into a small waterfall. Once, in a burst of vanquishing bravado, he'd climbed up and through that waterfall, following with a clear faith the steps of a companion. It was a feat struggling against the torrent of water; any faltering step might mean serious injury, if not death---the rise was not sheer, but strait---and he got to the top with an unaccustomed holler of glee. The others waiting below had not believed it could be done, but he had found it impossible to evade the implied dare of the leader as he scrambled up. It was true he'd been something of a daredevil as a kid, but that was when he didn't know better; here he knew his glory came as a result of unworried courage, the courage of trust. Who had once written that it was more fruitful to lose an illusion than to find a truth? And he could not tell which had happened on that waterfall afternoon---or had both? Soaked and with a pounding heart, he had reached down to pick up a shining pebble from the stream and, as if a gene from Primitive Man lurked secure in him, rubbed it dry in the sunlight and dropped it in his pocket.

8

As he stood there shuffling the old images in his head he noticed a diminutive canoa rolling about in the lagoon, maneuvered by two boys not ten years old. It was safe to practice in the sluggish lagoon, and no doubt the canoa had been built for that purpose. It would be frivolous in the bay on all but the calmest of days, and dangerous in the ocean. But the boys were laughing and taunting each other as their thin brown arms pulled at the oars furiously, standing at opposite ends with boyish insouciance and a grace not yet awkward. It was innocent frolic, *play*, to them; the *practice* was for their fathers. He wondered if his own son would take to it if given the chance. The canoas that ferried the tourists to the beach from the launches---and returned them later---were many times larger, and manned with vigilant skill.

He turned back into the restaurant and sat down at a table near the bar, away from the boisterous group in front, which showed no signs of leaving. It was also a table from which he could see Becky before she saw him. What was the advantage? Did he care that much? Or did he not want *her* to think that he cared that much? Amused at the game he seemed to be playing---but games made a pursuit more fun---he leaned around and ordered a beer

32

from a woman behind the bar. She was Steve's wife, Angelina, a pleasant and plump woman, much younger than Steve but not looking so, and she gave him a surprised and friendly greeting. They exchanged the usual small news of family and recital of dates, but many chores remained, they could chat later, at the Club de Yates in the village, which she also ran. He said it was good to see her, he hoped Steve was well, and took his second beer back to the table. Even without a watch he knew that the boats would be rounding the point soon, since the men were already hauling the canoes down to the shore from their berth on the upper dune. They were twenty or twenty five feet long, and hewn from a single trunk of parota, like the tree by his house, and so heavy that it was only a matchless determination that got them to the water. How else could they bring in their livelihood? Rowing machines of flesh and blood, the stalwart fathers leaned against the gunwales, waiting.

As he studied the menu to see if there was anything new, he heard the first boat hoot into the bay with drum flourishes from the small band on board. This was the Guadalajara Fiesta, though local wags called it the Dairy Queen. Arriving at 11:00 it would blast its horn at 2:00 or so to call back the flock, scattered in restaurants or riding horses in the jungle, or visiting the giddy waterfall behind the village, the one below the pipelines. Where was Becky? He didn't want to order another beer, and it was too early to have lunch, though the variety of fresh fish he'd seen slithered in ice melt in the back was enticing. Had she gone straight to her portrait commission? Changed her mind or forgotten? Before he could decide what to do, he saw a figure emerge from a small hut beyond the restaurant, dragging one leg, that came straight to his table to sit in a delicate slouch. Melman had a knowing grin on his face, but said not a word as he flung down a hefty, smudged notebook and sprawled back in the chair. He was barefoot and wore faded pants, the cuffs rolled up tight on his shins revealing a deep scar on one, and a torn shirt unbuttoned to the navel. Fierce brown eyes darted from a pale leathern face;

the fingers leather too, once elegant. They glared at each other as if playing some game of chicken, and it took a tidy minute before Melman announced, in a bark of triumph, that he had decided to live right on the beach. It was much better that way, simpler to live in a bare hut with a cot and a candle, and just 'scrounge on the universe', as he put it, jerking up an arm in a crooked salute. It was a gesture of inimitable finality, inflected by staccato chortles that rose emphatic in crescendo to a demonic cackle. Then he grabbed up the notebook and riffled through the pages, displaying a series of abstract squiggles or sketches that, he said, would define that universe; they'd occupied him deliriously for weeks. He'd even sold some to a woman at the hotel, and she was quite enthusiastic, promising to show them to an art dealer friend of hers when she got back to Los Angeles. But, he stammered, he needed no incentives; he was at the peak of his life.

As he listened, it seemed to him that Melman could not have been more pleased than if he were Einstein formulating at last the decisive theorem of a Unified Field Theory. But Melman didn't ask him what he thought, because he was much too satisfied with himself to need to know, and all his years in the village had not diminished his dogged nature. A hank of hair dropped over one eye as he jabbed an arm, almost growling in excitement.

He was a hemophiliac, and the bad leg was the result of a freak accident with a cable car in San Francisco. In the hospital, where there'd been trouble stopping the bleeding, certain botched procedures apparently occurred, and after protracted lawsuits or claims, he had finally come out with both a settlement and disability payments from the State. He had been a small business entrepreneur, and clever, but money went farther down here in Mexico, and he had important work to do. He'd known Melman since a few years before, when he lived in a large palapa in the village, and used to cook up a big pot of clam spaghetti for his friends with choice items brought down from California. But something had happened to him, because for some time his mind had gone threading into a wispy region of arcane musings, and his

last girlfriend Kristan, after a long inexplicable evening of lurid
mayhem, had tried to throw him out of the house. But by then
he was bleeding, so someone would have to arrange for him to be
carried down the hill to the beach, where a panga could speed him
off to a doctor in the resort town. She had come in the middle of
the night to his house for help, beside herself with guilt and fear.
He calmed her down with mild sex in the hammock, and at dawn
they went to find the *cargador* One Eyed Luis, and arrange for a
boat. Melman survived this tribulation, just as he had survived
the five days he spent in the resort town jail for failing to renew his
tourist card. In fact, he said he'd had a wonderful time there.

He liked some of the drawings, and thought their sinuous
lines, curls and shadings had an unexpected living force and
suavity, inhabiting a world strikingly different from the one of
usual, picturesque watercolors done by facile expatriates. He
thought them finer than Becky's, though he knew he would
not say so. As he looked at the notebook, Melman raved on
with his newest theory of Reality, just developed thanks to living
practically under the stars. And he would jab at one drawing
after another to make his point clear. Of course it was not clear,
though the ingenious twists of his patter was intriguing. Was it
folly and madness, woven finely, superseding sense? He could
not say. As he looked through the tumbling pages he wondered
at how he was always drawn to artists and painters, and they to
him, and a lot of his women had been artists. He lost his virginity
to one, when he was sixteen. Women of the word did not tempt
him nearly as much, though they made even better friends. Was
it because artists were always seeing what they looked at, and not
just going off with tangled mind as he did? Or that you could
talk to someone drawing, but not writing? He appreciated how
artists could put something down on paper that did not have
to be explained away by meanings: their test was in a different
realm. Musicians were like that too, but he had always been a
little intimidated by them, worrying that his own abilities might
get shown up.

And then Becky stood there, holding a tote bag in which he could see a large sketchbook. Another artist. She looked uncertain but determined, strangely peevish, and shifted on her feet. "So, you are hanging out...and with Mel", she shot at him, but he quickly saw that Melman himself was not exactly the cause of her irritable mood change. He decided not to reply, but to see what she would say next. It was Melman who continued to talk, trying to finish a tricky explanation, but now in a more soothing voice, dampened if not cowed by her presence. She continued to stand there, looking around as if to see who else might be there. She waved her arm scornfully toward the loud tour group at the front table, but then gave a forgiving gesture that seemed to include him. Doing one of her priceless pirouettes, she sat down in the chair nearest to him, and gave him a quick peck between lips and cheek "Oh, still you are drawing", she warbled to Melman across the table. He didn't answer her either, but gathered up his things in a huff and let it be known that he had an interesting appointment at the hotel, allowing little doubt about what it might concern, and dragged himself away. He heard him resume chuckling a little distance off, as though he'd remembered some cosmic joke that would not fit the tame size of their comprehension.

Without asking, he called out to a boy behind the bar to bring two beers, but felt her hand on his arm to tell him she did not want to drink before working, she would have a mineral water instead. He changed the order for himself as well, and watched her fumble in the tote bag, without bringing up anything. In a long filmy skirt over a bathing suit, she looked far prettier than in the morning, and her eyes were a darker, greener blue than before. She had this changeable quality about her, a fluctuating magnetic attraction to him---- eyes, moods, attention, interests: changing in the wind like clouds. Though she had kissed him on the cheek, he still could not guess her secret. What did she really expect from him? He thought it was enough that he was alone and she was alone, as if on a 'desert island', even while clamoring people waded ashore and began to crowd the restaurant.

"We should order soon, before the tourists do", he said, and she clapped her hands in assent. When the bottles came, he asked what kinds of fish they had, and settled for a whole, grilled mackerel. Becky wanted *quesadillas*. A confident breeze blew through the palapa, and they were content for a while to sit there quietly and watch all the unfolding, shapeless dramas of people arriving at an unfamiliar place. Happy, bewildered, angry, wily, petulant or inconsolable, each one carrying a burden of individual purpose, if not quite vision, which did not conceal the wish at least for coping with the life that was given. Given by what? They were milling about at random, as virtually unaware of each other as they were of the blue dome that towered over their heads. For a time they did not know where to go, but there were hawkers and hustlers to tell them. This one with a menu, that one with a horse, others with stacks of serapes or sombreros, and the girls with trays of pies that grew lighter every minute. A small boy held up an enormous iguana tethered by a string: a peso a photo. It was tiresome but someway fascinating to watch this daily fuss of the visitors, knowing how every day they inscribed their nameless names on the wheel of time in the village, and provided a large measure of its glad sustenance. Wasn't this what made each day almost wholly resemble its predecessor? There was a large and long "history" which had bypassed the village entirely but for a few relics of it: images of a benevolent or bleeding Christ. And was it complacent or reductive to believe that here the chain of life could not be known farther back than the memory of the oldest inhabitant? In that memory he knew there was a time of no visitors, no nameless names punctuating the wheel that turned undisturbed in the sleepy little fishing village. And so it still was, but was now also a fishy little sleeping village. Some of these scrambling people would sleep over; some of them might never want to leave.

9

It HAD BEEN THAT way for him: he had not wanted to leave. That morning after the acid trip in the hotel, recovered from the night terror of the insects, they spoke wishful plans over breakfast, thinking it a dream that must fade with their return to city jobs. It did not fade: on another trip two years later, abundant in a rented house above the village, the wishful plans resolved to decision; the following year they discarded everything of the city and came back to live...and promptly conceived their son.....

Propped in silence as the restaurant filled with tourists, they glanced at each other hesitantly, as if waiting for the barometer to move. They watched like voyeurs a stout man wrangling with a woman sopping from the crashing wave that punished her ill-timed jump from the canoa. The wind was rising, and fresh little whitecaps began to froth in the water. A trifling conversation sprang up, bits of news of who did what and who went where. There were perhaps twenty or thirty hopeful or semi-permanent foreigners who lived in the village, whose foibles could not avoid being observed---as if the foibles of one were not the foibles of many. To most of them---including himself---the world beyond the bay was bemusing, or like a movie pointless with stale jokes. So it was not that world disturbing their thoughts; something else chafed out a tension between them. He wondered if it was other than erotic, elicited from the tentative air itself that seemed to hover oblivious of the breeze.

Their food came, and his fish sizzled superbly, crisscrossed with black marks from the grill. A few years ago, he'd gone fishing in the bay with his friend Cary, in Santos' old canoa. They slipped off the beach in front of the house and paddled out not more than a hundred yards into a school of the same mackerel, *sierra* to the locals. Barely getting their lines in the water, they hauled in one after another of the smooth yellow and silver-blue fish, a pound or two each. They quit after twenty or so, and just floated around in the water, mollified by delight. Seeing their luck, other men had quickly gone out in their boats to grab their own share, and that night, he supposed everyone would feast on sierra. They gave a dozen to Santos for his brood, and invited a few friends passing by for dinner, grilling them on a stick over hot coals outside. Now he washed one down with the last of the mineral water, and started on the basket of tortillas and fresh salsa, while Becky picked at the quesadillas. She seemed still distracted and not very hungry. Looking at him more soulfully than he expected, she talked of her 'commission' and the 'groovy' payment she would get, and said she hoped he would share it with her later. She let her hand fall softly on his arm and, squeezing it lightly, rose with a sigh from the table. He smiled back, and said he'd come up to her house at sundown---okay? Yah, fine, we can make together some food. Then she pulled some pesos from her tote bag and dropped them on the table, saying she hoped it was enough, and went out the back into the bright afternoon.

A few minutes later, he saw her in the distance, demurely raising her skirt to wade across the lagoon to the far side, where Mariana lived. A white egret lifted a leg as she passed, breaking its shadow. The receding figure reached the path that went by Ruby's wide garden, and then he could no longer see her. *A figure in the distance, wading through a tropical lagoon.* It was an emblematic image that he held in his mind like a template, but he was aware that some element was missing---but what? An emblem not only of rampant nature, but of that alchemy of mind anxious to find meaning in life everywhere. The measure of man and the measure of the stars was the same, he read once. And the solitude of man was the solitude of the planets. The silence within him was firmer for the noise around, and the afternoon had an opacity through which he could barely see. Every object in the landscape of the lagoon seemed engaged in some airy struggle, and it was this conflict that he strove to grasp. There was not harmony, but an intricate polyphony perplexing to follow, boldly conjured but not heard, unlike that time of the night insects. And he imagined that every particle of sand, to the eye blending into one color, might give out its own sound of vitality, its own vibration of song, with no concern for his confusion. Yet was it clear: the ecstasy powering all things in the world could not be altered, nor could their sorrow be avoided. And the lagoon with its now imagined wading figure---the bay, the mountains, heat-blurred in the background---appeared like a landscape that had been forever waiting to be seen, and it was only he whose heart cried out for some sudden, decisive---*impossible*---clarification. How could it seem so hollow a hope with so much beauty blushing for itself all around? Convivial one moment, disjunct the next, he felt besieged inside himself, a sanguine occupant of his own body, with its vain knowledge and insidious chemistry. There would be no help without abdication to the ecstasy and the sorrow; somewhere in the middle inches of the mind might he learn the healing alchemy, and the vitality of his own sound had to be solely in his heart. It was as though he traveled on a highway that joined few towns, its loneliness stultified by a flickering, unsolved mystery---but only the unsolvable mystery was edifying. He thought that if he could sing like a *meistersinger* he would find the worthy prize at the end, not secret but enshrined in the soul of that deepest music where the mystery becomes a joy and no longer a taunt.

Exiled by temperament into his own imagination, he felt the afternoon going by in a loitering stream, now sparkling, now limpid; now dancing, now dozing. So if he would not let Time master him here, neither would he see it in ruins.

A restoring dip in the bay; another beer with idle conversation; in a beach chair, the last session of watching the canoas remove sated bodies from the beach to their excursion boat. The sun had plunged lower, routing the restaurant with its broil, blinding him. Only the huge, deep palapa of the Hotel Lagunita offered much shade, but he thought it was time to leave the beach; Steve had not shown, so there would be no chess. As the last boat rounded Pelican Rock out of sight, the workday of the *wheel* was nearly done; the recuperated calm was luscious, and the loss of hustle palpable.

He headed up the river on the left bank, past the soccer field, well past the last houses of *rentistas*, where the path narrowed to a trail. This was the rockier side of the river, less fecund, and the far-separated huts were the dwellings of poorer families, or hardier ones. Here, the source of water was only the river itself. He was thankful to breathe again the quiet air in the village outskirts, where twisted and tangled trees provided intermittent shade for his ramble. A modulated sun flickered through their gray and lichened branches. He could no longer hear or see the bay, and a different world was revealed. Twittering and rustling in the mixed shadows and glitters, a life less affected by the ocean emerged, and even the birds had a more furtive look in their flitting. It seemed as though a treachery lurked everywhere, and everything was aware of it. Without the rhythmic sounds of the bay, the tiniest voices were poignant, and the mesh of dispersed plants and animals more intricate. Abruptly from silence, a startling noise burst out as the great flock of sea birds that rested on the river by day rose and flapped off toward the bay. They would fly far as the islands, perhaps ten kilometers, to feed or roost. They climbed in slow flight calling to each other, cries whose plaintive echoes caromed in the river track for exquisite minutes. Or had they too just been waiting for the retreat of those boats? Often, in his house, absorbed in some task, or reading, oblivious even of the horn's blast, he would hear the cries of the seaward flock and know that the boats had gone. Their flight left echoes too in his heart that never wholly quieted, alloying the image of the lagoon with the sound of the flock. So it was this element missing from the template!----these birds; gulls, terns or plovers, which name he did not know.

10

BARELY SHELTERED UNDER THE sparse foliage of a blighted tree, he leaned against the paling of a slashed corn plot and watched them go, cleaving to the sound of their singular cawing. He thought he could hear a plea for forbearance in their cries, and felt someway a vindication---of what he could not tell. There was an old knowledge in the winging troupe, and he imagined it carried along more than bird knowledge; if its burden seemed fateful, the prophecy was cryptic. He would not *rather kill a man than a hawk*, as Robinson Jeffers had written, but he loved the flock, possessively, as if he wanted to own its bravura. The lengthening black shadow of a post merged with his in the fallow corn, pointing up the river toward the solemn, unreachable mountains, stark as the shadow cast by a gnomon, but one serenely unmarking, telling time only to those who knew it already ---or as if it gave a warning instead of the hour. But how much difference was there, after all.... if you can't *tell* the difference what *is* the difference? The birds were gone---for now---distant specks in the untouchable blue, printing a searing trace in his spirit; the afternoon was no longer young.

He resumed his ramble up the river path, too narrow for two, and came with no surprise to the *rancho* of Octavio, the young fellow who'd made his gate and mounted the new roof on his house. The compound had only a few small palapas and a tiny corral. His wife Leticia hailed him from the cool murk of the house, telling him that Octavio was way up the river, cutting wood for a new palapa he was building, and offered him a cup of water. The words of country Spanish flowed from her mouth like strains of folksong, and came from a gladness untroubled by scruple. A thought shot through his head: this was the center, the navel of the world, the village was on the outskirts---but the silliness of it made him cringe. When they were building his roof, he would sometimes come up here with Octavio in the afternoon, to share a family meal of tortillas and beans, and other things he said were gathered from the vicinity, more or less in the wild; a bowl of shredded meat was from a *tejon* easily shot between its gleaming eyes at night. The names meant little to him, but he could remember their textures and tastes. He'd learned his naïve Spanish from people like these *campesinos*, and was fluent only with them. Their children scampered around, laughing or grave, with naked feet and unclouded eyes. It was not just that what these people looked at, they *saw*---like artists---it was that, in his presence at least, they would look not behind, where schemes and calculations circulated, but before. So unlike himself, he knew, and so unlike his own people.

He thanked her, and left a greeting for Octavio, then continued walking up the river, but soon veered across it toward the right bank, tripping over the shining boulders strewn in the bed, not far below the waterfall. Only a middle course was running; the cold water splashed his feet, and the sibilance of its flow, now that he was in it, brought to his ears another water sound, unlike the roll of waves on sand, or resound on rocks. It was the insistence of water playing out a destiny it must have foreseen, as if charged to spread flotsam from the heights, like messages from afar, with neither pause nor rest. Its will, if such it could have, overcame all obstruction by rocks and debris without effort, and spoke in little voices, not all apparently accidental. In the waterfall, the river exulted; in the lagoon, it dawdled; reaching the ocean, it dozed.

He scrambled over the rocks onto the lush right bank, where the path was wide and the landscape expansive, making his way through Benino's grove of bananas, where gaudy fruit dangled in the sun and fantailed leaves jostled in irritation, goading tropical appetites. The doddering form of a *guanabana* tree appeared before him, with its spiky green fruit pendulous in the branches, some a foot long. When ripe, they whopped the ground in a sickening second, bursting open and spilling their thick, soft flesh into the dirt; stinking, but sweetly delicious. He went on through the clearing under the same old stand of coconut palms, tossing in the wind, whose high fronds blistered in the afternoon sun, as if awaiting deliverance. Then he passed the dense garden of Ruby's vegetables and flowers, a garden she worked and protected with the zeal of the dedicated expatriate. It was her lover Umberto who had built the bridge in town in his penance, and she would not bring herself to renounce him. And was it only a few hours ago that he had last seen Becky, passing along this same garden to her appointment? Where was she now?

With this question, he felt all at once satiated by the wildness, by the intemperate jungle, and he longed for a respite, a simple diversion. Without apology, he wanted to find his own flaws or foibles reflected comfortably in others, or deflected by them. And at the same moment, he saw that he was standing right in front of the twiggy gate and the winding steps of Maggie's house, she of the binoculars. By the gate's latch---this one store-bought--- a string zigzagged up a hundred feet through loops fixed on branches to the house, where a small bell rang. Though she monitored fastidiously the persons allowed to visit, she was averse to being alone, and surrounded herself with companions, guests or retainers. Hers was a narcissism that saw too faint a reflection in a mirror, and so she was avid for reflection to be given to her by them. Was this a judgment? Perhaps, he thought, but if so, he was judging himself as well, for he was now seeking a reflection too, one of corroboration, if not plain affirmation. His hand hesitated by the cord, steeling himself for rejection. More than once over the years he had pulled the cord, heard the ring, heard muffled laughter, but heard no invitation. Sometimes it was because she had customers, trolled from the beach or village by a confidant, and led to her lofty domain for instruction. Other times, how could he know? And he wished it didn't matter.

He gave the cord a decisive yank, and heard the bell ring with more fury than he had intended. Howls came up from her pack of dogs, which he had forgotten about, and an assortment of muzzles clamored out from the edge of the floor, madly barking down at him. One or two heads also peered out, but finally Maggie herself leaned over the edge and called out *"Quien es?"* Who's there? Before he could answer, she recognized him and shouted down the invite, reminding him to re-latch the gate so Xochi wouldn't get out. He began the climb, past spilling bowers of *bougainvillea* and thick bushes of *copa de oro*, to the house, trying to remember who Xochi was. As he reached the top he heard a horse whinny, and remembered: her pony.

"Well, hello there, the stranger returns, looking pale", she said, leaning over at the threshold, dressed in a long, profusely brocaded *huipil*, with nothing covering her thin legs; cigarette smoke curled from her fingers. Maggie was spindling, even gaunt, with a stooped posture, but her bearing was yet proud and unforgiving. They exchanged the usual cheek kisses, and she looked closely at him with a smile, saying, "You've put on some weight! I see the beginnings of a *panza*." "The food in California is more extensive than it is here", he answered, noticing the pony standing off to the side. Maggie's house was actually several large palapas connecting up the hillside, of which the top one was her bedroom. Between the roofs, a *jacaranda* cascaded in the flagrant purple of its bloom. She was unwilling, or unable, to keep the number of her "pets" down, so numerous dogs and cats lounged or scampered about the floors and garden of the house. He heard a chicken clucking somewhere in the brush outside. The pony seemed to have the run of the house too, and he had never asked how that worked out, nor had she ever offered explanation.

11

"You've been away for a while. How long is it?" But she waited for no reply, and walked back to the table, where Jarvis and his wife were each sitting absorbed in finger work. The table was at the other end of this front part of the house, clearly placed by a large gap in the luxuriant garden growth, through which much of the beach could be seen below. The binoculars were hanging on a hook nearby. As he neared the table, Jarvis put down his work and got up to give him a jovial greeting, laughing in his deliberately gruff manner. "You're just in time, we're trying out some new *mota* Enrique brought us from Tuito", he boomed, and shook his hand with both of his. A leather vest sheathed his bare chest, and his shaved scalp gleamed like burnished bronze. Mary Faith said hello too, but did not put down her work, which involved detailed sewing repairs to a garment. All around, textiles were neatly stacked on chairs and small tables, and there were many hanging on hooks screwed to the upright posts which supported the vigas. Mary Faith was in a huipil less elaborate than Maggie's, and her upswept hair reminded him of a woman's magazine ad from the turn of the century.

He waited for Maggie to sit down, but she had gone into another room, still talking, so he settled in the chair that looked sturdiest. The floor was mere sand, where fleas idled until any warm leg entered their neighborhood. Jarvis had also sat down, resuming his work on the rough stems and leaves fragrant in a square pottery dish. A meticulous job, picking out the twigs and throwing them aside on the table, then shaking the dish so the seeds rolled to one edge, from where he scooped them out onto the floor: "Chickens'll find them", he laughed, "before the *federales* do." Soon he had just leaves and resinous buds, and crumbled them to roll thin cigarettes from the pile. His fingers were thick and calloused, the instruments of a dexterous craftsman, and he earned his living by fashioning unique shoulder bags out of leather and rosewood, with odd bits of silver or stone worked in, which often were ordered by the customers who bought Maggie's huipils. Such work he claimed was the only therapy. He and Mary Faith lived on this same hillside, a tiny hut only a dozen yards away, and they were often at her table.

As Jarvis fired the first joint from the small line-up assembled, Maggie came back into the room with a bizarre wood sculpture in her hands. "Russell missed this one", she cackled. "Trudy won't let him stay at Na Bolom anymore, she says he's too commercial, too greedy. He couldn't see the gift horse staring him in the face," she sniffed, and set the thing down on the table. It was something like a mask, but much too large and unwieldy to be a danced mask from any Indian group. It had no holes for cord attachment. Anyone wearing the thing would need it supported by a brace, or an assistant. It was, in a word, grotesque, and had been further embellished with a white pigment rubbed all over to give it a look of sincere age. He knew more than a little about these things, and it failed to impress him. "*Very* interesting," he said, hoping they would catch the doubt in his voice without suspecting that he really had one. The joint was passed to him, pungent with fumes, and he took a lungful gingerly, but held it in as long as he could. Pot was the common lubricant for loosening tongues among the village expatriates, virtually de rigueur for conversation, and he thoroughly enjoyed it. The slight hesitation was due to his sharper anticipation of smoking some with Becky that evening. But now it was for social commerce and, feeling the glow come on, he asked innocuously where she had found this object. "Well, this Lacandon who brings things from the jungle to Trudy had a whole collection of them, but Russell happened to be there at the same time, and just laughed at them. What does he know? I told you, Trudy won't let him stay there anymore. I bought them all", and she pointed to a room behind the kitchen where he could go and see them. (Trudy was the widow of Franz Blom; the house in Chiapas bore his name in Maya.) Trying to conceal his reluctance, he got up and went to look. Sure enough, the room behind the kitchen was a kind of chapel, and on the broad back wall of whitewashed *lodo* were a group of ten or a dozen mask-like wood sculptures, hanging above and around a high table, festooned with paper cutouts of devils and skeletons, on top of which a large group of religious icons and other objects was arrayed. In the center of the altar, pride of place was taken by a large confectionary skull topped by a crucifix. He knew he was looking at a Day Of The Dead altar, though it was weirdly only spring. He stood there, weighing what effort he'd make to ease himself out of the flattery and admiration he was sure she wanted. So this was the reflection he had sought when he emerged from his walk up the river---and what did he expect? But then he admitted to himself that perhaps he was not as certain of the doubtful provenance of these objects as he pretended, and he knew that Maggie had a strong eye for the crafts of the Indians. He considered her even as a mentor, for she had encouraged his early ventures. But no…No. He *was* certain they were bogus. They were not dance masks, they were freelance decorations, another category altogether. He had learned about masks from that same Russell, who had gathered a collection in the Forties, traveling on horseback in the mountain villages and ranchos of southern Mexico. Not that he was so in love with truth that he was incapable of being unfaithful to it by embracing the false. He returned slowly to the table, not in a hurry, in time to receive the joint again, and took another slow drag, buying time, thinking himself a coward. "I think you've found something quite unique," he announced with the exhalation of smoke, "really *unusual*." He handed the roach to Maggie, who declined, and then to Jarvis, who flashed him a quick look of what might have been relief; Jarvis relished only his own disputes. Mary Faith's fingers paused in their work, and she said, without looking up, "They're not for sale." Suppressing a guffaw with a cough, he felt the effects of the grass, but it had not put him at ease. Unable to think of anything else to say, he wandered carelessly around the room, inspecting some of the items on display. He stopped by a clutch of net shoulder bags that came from a certain village in Guatemala. He loved them, and it was he who had brought the first group to Maggie from there. She bought all the ones he offered, and for several years he maintained his larder out of this small trade. The one he carried now was the same, hanging in back of his chair, but from use the yellow strands had burnished to rich butterscotch. These bags helped define the fashion that Maggie, with imposing personality, made essential for gringos in the village, and together with the ethnic clothes, compelled a chic as snobbish as anything on Fifth Avenue. Sooner or later, most of the expats from New York, Aspen, Sausalito and Santa Monica appeared in the garb; their need for initiation provided Maggie with a lifestyle of hauteur. Jarvis and Mary Faith---and he himself---were following in her footsteps. His first strides had been solely for the sake of survival, since the instincts of a merchant were born in him. Now he was more interested in the arts of those peoples than in their costume, a subtle distinction that allowed him to quietly, even secretly, revel in his own recondite hauteur.

12

THE HOUSE WAS DARKENING as the sun slipped behind the village, though a glare shimmered up from the farthest beach. There were still a couple of hours of daylight left, but a chillier dusk would prevail in the village for what remained. He thought of the cool shadows in his house now, but sat down at the table again, hoping the graceful time for departure would soon occur. Whatever was the reflection he had longed for, it had not come. He could not help feeling a confusion of applause and aversion for these people, and he indicted himself for feeling so conflicted. Where was its reason, really? Doing a little digging might find his own fault in it, though he knew he could find incidents of their making to fault as well. And why look for fault? He didn't care why, since things came into his mind that he could not ignore or excuse. With a nursing infant of her own, his wife had been summoned late the night Mary Faith birthed a boy without even the help of Esperanza, the village midwife. There was some trouble, Donna was an obstetric nurse, so the summons had been realistic. Of course he had stayed with their infant, and paced the floor worrying about what he would do if he awoke, hungry. Whatever the problem, it persisted overnight, probably a result of

Mary Faith's sheer stubbornness. She was determined to have a child au naturel. No one had lifted a finger---as his mother would say---or even paid a visit, during Nico's first months.... There was the strenuous abusiveness of Jarvis when he was drunk on the local, cheap *raicilla*. Then, he bluffed a preference for provoking irritation and discomfort rather than disarming them, acting the irascible artist. He and Jarvis had gotten drunk together a few times, and the heartless rancor he directed at other people, both absent and present, seemed like it should be an affront to him as well. But it wasn't. Or he would not allow it to be. Instead, he let it amuse him, something to observe without reaction, in a forgiveness of 'genius'. Well, there was no shortage of fault to find, and if he had sought a reflection, a corroboration, in visiting Maggie after his hour of wildness up-river, maybe he had found it, after all..... Human relations in virtuous or vicious circle, and all ran round inside them.

Maggie had made some coffee while he was spinning in these thoughts, and he realized that they had all been chatting meanwhile, ignoring his abstraction. Then he also realized how stoned he was, and how stoned they were, but the finger work continued, while Maggie was looking through the binoculars toward the beach. "Well, Becky's looking good these days", she wheezed, "I haven't seen her for a month. I worry about her. I hope she's getting what she needs....I hope she knows what she needs." And she handed the binoculars to Jarvis: "Take a look." He grabbed them, and muttered, without looking, "Oh, you know what these high strung women with sketchbooks are like, relieving boredom with pretension, wondering why they're not happy in paradise." He jabbed the binoculars out dismissive---daring anyone to look--- as though he wanted to make it clear that *his* attention would be deflected only by matters, or persons, of invincible consequence. He thought the gesture fitting but was too unnerved by it to take them, though he wanted to see her. Jarvis sputtered on, his eyes brimming with smart condescension. Deep wrinkles furrowed his brow while ashes fluttered like gnats from his beard.

A graceful time for departure had not come, but knowing that Becky was walking home from the beach gave him an impetus for action, but while he pondered making a move, Mary Faith, in the measured tones of her manner, said, "She should put her mind to something more practical, and stop that mooning". She had hardly looked up from her work, and her long face showed no expression. This comment annoyed him more than any other, and he jumped up from the chair and announced, knowing before the words left his mouth how foolish they might sound, "Sometimes, there's poetry in mooning; not everyone can be practical", and he took pains to pronounce the last word with the utmost sarcasm. It seemed to have the desired effect, since not a word passed anyone's lips for a few minutes, and mirth was in suddenly short supply. Finally, Maggie got up and called out, "Santiago! Come and play us a tune," as she walked over to a hammock in a far corner of the room, giving a shake to the figure in it. He had not noticed that Santiago was in the hammock, Maggie's sometime foreman or lover, and he began strumming a few plangent chords on a *guitarron,* the bass guitar lying on his stomach, in a minor key as if to mirror the prevailing mood. The man was tall and striking, with a laconic knowingness in all his movements, not one of which ever seemed wasted or clumsy. Of an indeterminate age, but not young, he had the look of mysterious power that a shaman might have. Once, Maggie had told him, he dispatched a scorpion by stepping on it though barefoot: *he knows the way,* she whispered. And, as he was still standing after his outburst, he stepped over in Santiago's direction and nodded his head in hello, then returned to the table, finally willing to take his leave, mumbling and receiving the dutiful pleasantries of goodbye. Then, amidst a renewed but now perfunctory barking, he went down the steps to the path, pausing a minute, listening to the song Santiago began to intone.

He went through the gate and turned to latch it back, so Xochi couldn't get out. The light was a relief. On the path, a

complex wave of----what?...feelings?... thoughts?... emotions?----
washed over him: satisfaction, doubt, amusement, elation, regret
for spoken comments and unspoken ones, and finally, a sense
of business concluded, leaving him breathing freely and fully,
without the restraint of the rarefied domain above. He knew that
if he had felt restrained it was his failing, not theirs. So he walked
ahead jauntily, up the path, which now passed the ugly concrete
cellblock that Victor was building in stages, just off the stagnant
sidewaters of the lagoon, whose rooms were rented to those who
were too lazy or ignorant to make it up the hill and into the
village. But he was being too harsh, since a year ago he'd had a
girlfriend who lived there, and, once inside, it was not bad, the
beach could be seen, and the sweet sound of waves heard.

The rise of the path brought him again to that spot overlooking
the whole bay and river, where he stood that morning and the
night before. It had a vantage classical in postcard archives, and
was a natural pivot point; coming or going, he would always pause
to sweep the scene, like the reconnaissance of a scout, delving at
the divide between personal and public choices.

A pack of children ran up the steep path from the beach, and
practically ran into him. They were wildly laughing as they shot
ahead faster on the level way to the village. Watching them, he
thought, at first abstractedly, of his own childhood, measuring
their rapture against what he remembered of his own. Differences
emerged at once, though it was not as if that made a difference. But
he saw that his public version of childhood was of a happy one, and
as he looked deeper, he found more troubles and anomalies than the
public version could accommodate, for that version turned out to
be more like his parents', one that required many blacked out lines
and paragraphs---if not whole pages to be cut. He shook his head
against these thoughts, partly because he did not want to have them
at all, but more likely because they interfered right then, and there,
with the perfect sense of being he was nurturing. Philosophical
angst was one thing, while psychological anguish was another. Take
the line of least resistance and for now be glad enough for it.

13

As HE WALKED IN a deliberate stride toward the village, such resisted thoughts of self-knowing still held his mind; there was not even pith and wit to enliven them, but the sort of banal fiction that is liable to stretch even a rigorous account of fact. Fiction to conceal a builded disguise---double the effort---making up the story wished for, but not the one lived. He forced his attention away and on to what he would buy in the *tiendas*. He should bring things for dinner to Becky, but did not know what she might have. A few stragglers from the pack of children had stopped on the concrete bridge, to catch their breath while still giggling. Against the blur of shoving and jumping kids he saw in a smiling flash the time when he'd emerged from a candy store clutching a 15-cent ice cream cone. After just a lick or two, the scoop 'jumped' out to the sidewalk, as if in perverse volition. With only a dime left in his pocket, he managed to push some back into the cone, heartsick. These kids had no ice cream.

He let himself think of nothing. In the shade of a mango tree heavy with ripening fruit a few men were idling beside a boiling cauldron of *chicharron*. A woman cradling a large cloth-covered basket received the crisp sheets; soon she'd go sell them on the bridge. A big scurvid dog tore at scraps between snarls at other hungry curs. He turned down a tiny side path twisting between some houses and came out behind the Club de Yates, a restaurant that sat up one side of the village beach, the landing used for local business. Almost all the goods brought from the resort town came in here, and the Club was a good place to watch the activity. Small passenger boats anchored there, including the old Lucinda. Everyone and everything came to and left from the beach by canoa or panga. At this hour there was not much activity, and the few people sitting in the Club were the ones he had seen rowing from the yacht that morning. A woman with two men and a boy sat at a table near the edge of the floor, where it dropped down to the rocks below. Without railing it was a naked drop, and more than one drunk had fallen at night onto them. There were a couple of others in the place, young trippers he did not know, so he went through and across the beach, jumped over the flagging creek and up the cemented ramp on the other side to the tiendas. The original owner of this "yacht club" was a character named Eye Patch Bill, whose own yacht had sunk, or *was* sunk, around the point, and he built the place with insurance money. Angelina had bought it from him, and now ran it with her teen-age children.

Four or five tiendas were steps apart in the village, open informally in front of the houses. Almost everyone was related by blood or marriage, and commerce thrived in a symbiosis similar to small villages the world over. Martin's brother had a boat that ferried goods in; Benino brought *raicimos* of bananas from his grove up the river to be sold in nephew Enrique's shop; Juan Cruz sold his coffee in daughter Etelvina's store, and it was her husband who managed the houses Cruz rented to gringos. *Etcetera*. Juan was like a godfather to many in the village, and though political office was not a conspicuous practice, little of consequence occurred without his approval. A village elder who seemed to manage affairs from a hammock off the sunny yard where the coffee beans were dried, he spoke a succinct Spanish, colored by the guttural accent of a native dialect apparently forgotten. He had been born early in the century in the mountains some miles away, where he grew the coffee. Juan also grazed cattle somewhere up the river, and every Tuesday in the corral behind the house a steer was slain in a crude shamble at dawn, and Juan used to save half-a-kilo of liver for his pregnant wife. The village was part of a *comunidad indigena* within the Mexican political system, and was reputed to have originated from a grant by the King of Spain himself, a century before Mexican independence. There was very little trouble in the village that required action by outside authority--- except for the *migracion*, nemesis of pot-smoking gringos---and the few incidents that were known to him had the luster of legend. Except for Juan Cruz himself, and a revolving deputy to the comunidad seat, the village existed without legislature, judiciary or executive. The lesson of the village was heightened by its unexampled combination of isolation and access, uniting a remove from modern life with an acceptance of the ramble of outsiders who were products of that modern life. The village was its own and yet not its own; the coexistence of two disparate peoples, felicitous entirely, by magic or grace, each informing the other. That it subsisted faithful to itself despite its dependence on the outsiders was a salient part of the lesson. He had not come, in the beginning, to learn any lessons, not yet knowing he did not know, but to live in untrammeled nature, to live apart from the modern world; to live as much untouched by the stupid persistence of a brutal war as possible. He knew he might be living a myth, but he wanted to live a myth, and considered it the noble choice, both personal and public. They had broken all ties to the city and heard the admonition to Turn On, Tune In, and Drop Out as a command. Really, it was as simple as that. And some of their city friends had already done, or would do, the same. *Ein, zwei, drei.*

He gathered into a pile some tomatoes and avocados, onions, chiles and cilantro from a table at the first tienda he passed, and brought them to the counter, a wooden shelf in a window. There, a churlish girl of twelve added up the purchase, which he dropped in his net bag and paid for. The next tienda had the best sweet, tawny *bayo* beans, and he bought half a kilo. These were wrapped in thick brown paper and given a cunning twist to keep it together, any sort of tape unknown. An older woman took his pesos, and smiled at him, because she was fond of his blond-headed boy; she was the postman's mother. Her mild husband was usually visible sitting inside the house, nodding his head, often with grandchildren crawling at his feet. Since he himself was between the young and the old, his sympathies hovered uncertainly between them: nubile girl or kindly woman---which? He laughed to himself at this trivial indecision, walking on to another store. There, on a rough wood table in a patio, was a neat pile of ripe papayas. He picked one of a medium size with inviting yellow and green tints, hoping it was red inside, brought it to be weighed, this time by an older girl, more poised than the first and a little flirtatious. A good papaya made a feast of any breakfast. Seeds tossed out his window sprouted, but failed to grow fruit. What else should he get? Juan Cruz had long ago sold out his supply of brown rice, taken from the house of a deported gringo, so the bland rice in his house must do. Some potatoes were left over too, should they need some. Another can of sardines. He went back to the tienda of the churlish girl, and bought one. It would do in a pinch. Retracing his steps, he passed by Eva's little beer hall, and she waved him on with her happy laugh. But a second thought took him back, and he bought four bottles of beer, which he thought could be kept chilled by immersion in the cold water from the sink. The little gas refrigerator he had brought down some years back was not hooked up, as its gas tank, missing for a year, had never been replaced. Being away from the house weeks or months at a time, even with others looking after it, had its hazards. Only Eva's older daughter was sitting at the table with her, and Eva was telling him, as he stuffed the bottles in his bag, what a good wife she would be for Nico in ten years. He joked with her, saying that he did not want Nico to get married until he was at least thirty, which would be too long a wait for Sarita, the daughter. This retort made Eva laugh gustily, and he slipped away while she recovered.

14

SQUEEZING BETWEEN BOULDERS AND tripping on tree roots, he traipsed back along the path, to the creek by Pipeline Jim's old house, where the white flowers of the datura were still closed, looking now virginal. He stood there, thinking they should open for him, and pinched off a spray for Becky, wondering if the trumpets would blare if put in water. As he reached his gate he saw, jolting down the path from the point, a grizzled old man riding a mule with a large glass jug roped on each flank. When he drew up, he knew they were 19 liter *damas* holding *raicilla*, the moonshine tequila made in Guasimas, near Chacala, seat of the comunidad, several thousand feet up in the mountains. One dama was empty already, and the other looked quite low. He would have to buy some, knowing the rounds the old purveyor made were haphazard. The trail back to Chacala went up right behind his house, so he felt lucky. He raised a hand wordless and went inside to get an empty bottle and brought it back also wordless. Without dismounting, the man pulled a cob stopper from the jug, tilting it way over to pour through a funnel into his bottle, splashing some on the ground. The smell was none too pleasant, but after a thoughtful swig he could tell that it was a pretty good batch, smooth and not too noxious. Made in old copper stills from the mashed heart of a smallish maguey, the taste was one you had to acquire. But with it you acquired a simular mystique as well, as if it bore the ancient repute of hallucinogens. Call it *sunshine,* more virile if not stronger than *moonshine,* untaxed so not legal, and, at a peso a snifter, you soon felt you were living the storied life of an outlaw, scoffing at those who imbibed from labeled bottles. He paid the man and offered him a swig from his bottle, which he declined with a wink of conspiracy like a tout, and spurred on the mule amidst parting laughter, indeed going up the trail to Chacala.

He carried the bottle to the kitchen and eagerly poured a few fingers into a glass, sliced a limon into seedless chunks, dusted them with salt, but realized the heavy bag was still pinching his shoulder, so he switched it to the nail on a post, then retrieved the glass and limon from the kitchen to sit down with a sigh at the table. But he remembered the beer, so he shot up again and took the four bottles from the bag and set them in a plastic *balde* filled with cold water, giving the little fridge a wistful glance. From the slope right behind the kitchen he heard a rustling sound, and suddenly a large cat appeared on the ledge of the retaining wall he'd built there. It was Tao, "his" tabby, and she was slung low with kittens. How many litters had she had? At least two a year for seven or eight years, and she was a wise old *madre* with sure jungle knowledge, who had survived very well with little human help. A gift from Santos when he lived just below, she was still a fisherman's cat, and knew just when to wait on the rocks below to get the leavings from cleaned fish. When he was here, she usually hung out with him. One of her most laudable traits was a stern refusal to tolerate any dog in the house, and he had seen her spook and chase off even a German shepherd. She came up to him on the kitchen counter, begging for his caress, and he was unsparing in his affection. They had a history between them, and they shared the history of others. She might come when he called and was often there on the beach when he arrived.

He knew that it was only her impending litter that had delayed her appearance this time, and he picked her carefully up. She nuzzled into his face, and he thought how strange it was to love this cat for her dog-ish qualities. He would save her a sardine if he opened the can, but he could see she was quite healthy. Few of the roaming cats and dogs in the village were. Her offspring were scattered around; even Maggie had one, a favored female named Moustache.

He put her down on the kitchen floor, but she walked to the front and jumped into his chair, so he pulled up another to drink the raicilla still waiting on the table. Swallowing fat fingers of it, the liquor quickened him with a screaming sapience that he knew was an illusion---but who did not love an illusion? Thin mythologies were fattened with illusions, and all political life could not thrive without them. Not to mention spiritual life. *More fruitful to lose an illusion than to gain a truth*? Perhaps that was misleading, because with a single truth many illusions at once were lost. Or was truth itself the ultimate illusion---or illusion the ultimate truth? He sputtered out a laugh, knowing that with another few swallows of raicilla his mind could go on for a wonderful while, playing games with words, revolving a theme and variations, like two hands wandering at will on a piano, if not quite unraveling there the theme of a genius caring not a fig for what you thought his meaning was. Why did meaning have to have a meaning? Rather, how could meaning *have* a meaning? Say the word "meaning", say it enough and eventually the word will say nothing, or will say *you*. When a word reaches as far as the lips, the mind can no longer pronounce it. Ah, with one more swallow, all questions will be mooted in the mystique of raicilla, adduced here on a seaside edge of mythic life.

He glanced up at Tao, facing him wide-eyed in the other chair. She looked as if she knew what he was thinking, puzzled but not surprised. She knew him too well, and, with the surely sublime patience of a cat, she knew it would pass. As he looked at her, she lifted her head to meet his gaze and they held it, together, in something that seemed like communion. She would not look away until he did, and that was a bond. And he felt, not strangely, that it was possibly the clearest bond, free of truth and illusion, and importantly free of words. Man of words, how could he crave freedom from them?

The light was going, and shadows began to climb in cool ripples toward the sky. There was only a bit of sunlight left on Pelican Rock out at the entrance, and the birds were there. Half an hour of daylight to go, and then the satin darkness of the village would be accomplished again, and the vigil for moonrise begun. Voices resounded from many directions, and the surf crashed below on the rocks in a vigorous wind. A panga rounded the Rock where sunlight blurred, and sped into the bay without cutting its motor, streaking to shore with an urgent noise that seemed tinny in the blowing bay. Probably the expected boat, though he knew not by whom. At this time of day, any boat would be expected, and there were no alarms raised. Was all well? How could it not be? Not a drop was left in his glass, and he was glad for the night coming. Stepping into the garden, he wanted to hear the faint crinkle of elephant ears in the wind. The strains of a sad bolero from a nearby radio he savored, and high up in the tree spreading over his roof he could see three or four large birds ruffling their feathers in company, quietly chattering. No doubt their language had meaning for *them*---therefore for *us*---and he thought that if the *process* of life was described in the verbs between the nouns, its *quality* was in the adjectives. He felt as talented for night as were the birds, and as unabashed by his thoughts as they seemed by theirs.

15

When the sun at last found the horizon, after finishing its hour long descent behind the mountain, daylight would fade quickly as if drained, so he went back to the kitchen where the lamps from night were lined up by the sink, blackened with soot. He knew the way of trimming the wicks neatly to prevent the blackening, but he had not bothered, so the glass globes had to be washed before lighting again. This he did with a brush while Tao stayed in the chair, her eyes almost closed. He could not tell when the kittens would come, but he recalled her first litter, when she was hardly more than a kitten herself. She was lying at the bottom of the down sleeping bag that he and his wife slept in the first year, and her look of surprise did not surpass his own. But she'd known exactly what to do, and when the tiny creatures were all squirming on the bed, she dragged them one by one to a corner in the house, where his wife had made a nest. It was night, but in the morning there they all were, licked clean and nuzzled into her belly, and Tao had that same look of surprise----or was it pride? The kittens---five or six---scampered around for some weeks and grew into a quick adulthood; most were given away, but one was just gone one day. Tao grew up too.

He lighted the lamps and set them around the house, charmed to see the white burn in each globe bewitch its place with a certain personality. As they were lighted, the world outside the house went all at once black, and only a limpid sky was glimpsed between the branches of the vast parota. The contours of the bay were muted, only later returned to the scene in moonlight. The wind died, and the tranquility into which the bay subsided seemed as if it could last forever. He grinned at thinking that if he held his breath, it would. But he took a breath sure enough, living for the flair and fun of it, for the wild night and the ineffable future. He remembered how his son had been slow to take his first breath, and for some agonizing, endless seconds in the little room at the Centro de Salud, he himself could not breathe, until he heard the tiny wail claim its life. It was very early Christmas morning, after a noisy Eve in the resort town. With that wail he became an amazed father, and in the coincidence he had thought of the willing forbearance of Joseph, bearded black as he himself then was. It had taken a couple of shots of pitosin to urge him out, and only later did he learn that the American 'doctor' had been an imposter, merely an Army medic. From the first breath in to the last breath out... acquiring a ghost, then releasing it... one ounce in, one ounce out. To the cosmos of the world the sigh of that last breath is only an instant after the first, as if life was little more than the moans and gasps, the squeals and fluttering, of a phantom, spent wholly in the specious imaginings allowed between those seconds ---yet even a second is eternal.

He took off his trunks, put on long pants, splashed water on his arms and changed his shirt, then repacked the net bag with some of the food and the four bottles of beer. He turned the lamps low and looked for the new, small flashlight he had brought. He gave Tao a little pat and went out the door, turning to the back gate that led to his beach. Once outside, it did not seem so dark, and he didn't really need the flashlight. From the corner of the house just above the beach, the path to the Point rose up immediately onto a boulder outcropping that formed a ledge, and the steps to

Becky's house began there. Like Maggie's, there was a cord with a bell and he pulled it, but could hear nothing, so he climbed slowly up. Halfway, he turned around to see the vista of the bay opening to a larger world, and the waves from this height were jouncing under feeble starlight, like a cartoon of rippling muscles on the flanks of a beast. Beyond the lagoon, the hotel sparkled with the lights from its generator, and lights were sprinkled on the village and hillside. As the scene *did* take his breath away, he drew in some air, and forgot about ghosts to muse instead about the different ways to read the phrase *out of time* as he exhaled. The stars born in the sky were southern stars, and thirty miles across the huge bay in which this was but a cove he could see the elusive outline of Punta Mita. There was no way to explain the scene, its weightless potency crucially deprived of words------though only the words of talk. There were other words---- firmer words, the strong words of Art, those that are provoked in us when we hear the perfected voices of imagined gods, that arrive like apparitions to goad the imperfect dictions of our plight.

With a few more steps he stood on the small patio beside the house, and illumination flickered warm inside. He whistled a signal as he got to the doorway, like his without a door, and heard Becky from inside:

16

"Ooh….nice….here you are," she cooed, "I've been touching up my portrait of Mariana, come and do a look."

The palapa was much larger than his, and propped in the middle was an easel with two brightly burning lamps around it; a candle winced bravely in the breeze. And it was almost without walls, except for the corner kitchen and another area with makeshift palm strips lashed outside, hanging fabrics inside, cleanly enclosing the bed. But the house was not on the main trail, and there were no others nearby, so it could be even more open than his. He came up to the easel where she stood pondering to give her a quick kiss, but she was absorbed in her work, and just kept murmuring "Eh, ah, yes, I… think so…huh?" Their shadows dodged in the palm patterns above their heads; with the more distant crash of waves on the rocks, insect sounds were less drowned out. He looked at the portrait she'd done that afternoon, and thought it striking. In a style he supposed was northern European, the pastel was a subtle and intricate study, whose subject was a plumpish Mexican woman, probably not more than twenty five but looking older, her cheerful face without guile as one hand rested on the shoulder of a small child who, in turn, was holding a kitten by the scruff, looking as if it had just been dragged from a skirmish. Rendered with tender skill, he imagined something like this on a sidewalk in Brussels, with Becky bent and prancing over it, prideful from the praise of passersby. But now she was deprecatory, smudging a line here, stroking a little color there, stepping back, staring hard, and muttering. On an impulse, charged with conviction too, he grabbed her free hand to stop its dismissive waving, and pulled it to his mouth, not so much to kiss as to bless it. Resisting his gesture at first, he felt her body relax through the arm, and she threw the crayon down on the table and turned to him. "Its not too bad... they liked it...look at the bag of pot he gave me", she whinnied, pointing at the table. "And there's a *goood* piece of fish in the fridge too" she added. Of course, she had one, he realized. Still clasping her hand, he drew her to him in a light embrace, and told her he thought the drawing was wonderful. She protested, mildly he thought, and said she wished he could see her sidewalk work. Their embrace tightened, and in a small voice told him how she had wished him to come alone, but had always showed up with a woman. And then she pulled away, dancing to the kitchen, and announced that she was starving, hadn't eaten since the quesadillas in the afternoon, did he know what to do with the fish. Surprised by her question, he went over to her, and said he was hungry too, let's make dinner. Retrieving the bottles from his bag he opened two and gave her one, stowing the others in the fridge.

Seeing the fish there, he took it out, saying he'd cook it if she did something with the rest. She had some decent rice, not just the dull starch of the Mexican variety, and he dumped out the vegetables from his bag in case she needed them. After putting on a pot of rice, she sat down to roll a joint. While he looked around the kitchen for a large frying pan, she was talking about some family situation in Antwerp that might call her back sooner than she liked, but hoped it would get resolved. He could hear in her voice the Flemish lowlands; like a mirage appeared a roomy kitchen steaming with the smell of simmering meat and fumes of kneaded dough rising warm in the pantry. Visible through the fogged window he saw fields of flowers through which files of anxious children were making their way home from church school. Towards the front was Becky, a thin, wan girl in a bonnet, fringes of flaxen hair showing, with a bounce in her step already. Soon he saw himself in a succeeding image as a boy sitting in his mother's cramped kitchen ----such a contrast!----at a formica table, with an unsightly sausage of gefilte fish before him, daubed with a pillow of horseradish luridly scarlet from infused beet juice. His aversion was overcome by the likeable taste. The icebox squatted in a tiny pantry, cooled by a block of ice carried in on the shoulder of the iceman, who cameth every Friday. And while Christ agonized above the Belgian cupboard, Moses wearily huffed from his Chicago redoubt. Cabbage and potatoes must have gone with the boiled meat, while his fish would certainly be followed by a chicken soup tangled in wispy veins of noodles, slippery as if to escape. And with this odd reverie in his head, he sliced a few limones to marinate the fish, which he happily saw was a thick slab of dorado from its golden skin, a fish even finer than the sierra of the afternoon. Hooked out in the large bay---a black void now---it was a spirited game fish, and he would give it a vigorous fry to vindicate such colorful resistance.

"Got any corn flakes or flour?" he called out to her, intent on rolling the joint; her effort looked desperate compared to Jarvis's.

"Yeah, look under the counter, I think there is some."

He bent down, but the deep shelf was dark, so he lowered a lamp carefully to peer inside where he found a box of corn flakes, just what he wanted. He dumped some out on a plate, then crushed and sifted them in his hands to a fine grain.

"How about an egg", he asked.

"On the counter in a basket----what do you do with it?"

"Use it all to fry the fish." And in the way she spoke the last phrase, the visions of their disparate childhood kitchens arose again, and he saw himself at one end of the formica table with his father at the other, third side against the wall, the last by the stove fitfully occupied by his mother, cooking and serving the courses of dinner: his anxious mother talking to his phlegmatic father, while his own head drifted in the clouds---a *luftmensch*, as she teased him sometimes. And Becky's? The contrast had intrigued him, but now his imagination was shuttered, and only his old childhood scene lingered, while he stood in the kitchen deftly skinning the fish, dousing it in the beaten egg, and coating it with corn flake dust. This was a jungle strategy his old friend Ken had shown him years ago, before he'd gotten deported for marijuana.

He put the fish on to fry at a high heat, and announced it would only take ten minutes. She glided into the kitchen with a clumsy looking joint in her hand, and gave it to him. "I'll make up some salad with what you bring", she sang, and busied herself. He went out on the patio to gaze at the thousand stars arrogant in the sodden air, an air so full they were blinking like lights in a penny arcade, and suddenly against the sky he saw the flap of a fruit bat swooping through the house. "Got a *raicimo* of bananas hanging in there?" he asked her, busy with the salad nearby. "A bunch in a basket here", she replied, and he told her to cover them, unless she didn't mind the bats. "Yeah, I forgot", and she threw a cloth over the basket.

A fresh breeze blew up then, and all the lights on hillside and beach winked crisp for the easing purpose of village life at evening. Limbs relaxed, children tired at last, there was food and drink to be savored, and laughter thrilled in converse. Like a predilection, strength rose in him with no surprise, and it flared with the sense of a moment, though similar to many another, that would implant some unique artifact in his consciousness---- to be vivified later ---on which he would rely to the end. ("How far are you going?" he was asked once by an acquaintance he encountered when riding his bicycle in Lincoln Park. "I guess to the end", the questioner answered himself.) He wanted to shout or stamp his feet, and this glee, like that of the night before, was beyond accolades: glee was the key to understand the world in a way that despair merely encumbered, for the atoms whirled only in glee.

On the ledge was a box of wax matches and he scratched one to light the joint, inhaling deeply, then took it inside where Becky was chopping the salad, and passed it to her, finger to finger. She stopped to take a hit, and coughed out the smoke with a burst of laughter----as if she'd caught his glee---- and pressed up to him with a coquettish grin, and said the salad was ready. He gave her a squeeze and went to the stove to flip over the fish, which was about to burn. She set out two plates and arranged the avocado salad on them, spooned in a little rice and some limon slices, and waited for the fish, which he halved in the pan and scooped sizzling onto the plates. They carried them to the table near the easel and, with a nod for ceremony, started right in.

She *was* hungry, and dug in with gusto, exclaiming how terrific the fish was, and he had to agree. The vivid struggle of the creature to keep its life in some way imparted to it a special quality, almost a nobility, and he felt a privilege in the partaking.

"Want some more beer?" he asked.

"I still have a little."

"The mota is very good. Where did you say it comes from?"

"I don't know, up the river maybe, Jorge has people in Tuito." She got the words out between mouthfuls, and was eating like an athlete. Dressed in another long skirt, he noticed, with a kind of smock over it, her eager manner was infectious, and he forked up a big chunk of the fish and crammed it down too. A cat wandered over out of darkness, looking up at them with diffidence, but lunged after the small piece of fish he dropped. He could not tell if it was one of Tao's kittens, but thought it probably was. Becky said something to the cat in Flemish, and it was as if a different person were there, no doubt the girl from the field of flowers he'd imagined. Even the way she moved changed, but as soon as she resumed in English, it was the same Becky.

She got up and went toward the bedroom to put a cassette in the machine she had sitting on a cloth-covered crate. It was

Dylan's *Highway 61 Revisited*, one of his own favorites. She danced a little to the music, then looked for the joint and re-lighted it. This time she held in the smoke before offering it to him. He took some in while still eating, and handed it back. She floated to the edge of the floor facing the bay, stretching her arms out like a prophetess, and sang along with Dylan's music, seemingly in her own world, for some minutes. He watched her in a pleasant haze, his thoughts in their own world too, now an intoxicated world jammed with words and phrases idly groping for some principle that might rule them. But the purpose warred with his blood, whose tide was clearly flooding to the feminine charm and energy displayed before him. His mind might be in no hurry, but his blood began to scream.

17

FROM THE EDGE OF the floor she leaned into the night and peered through the fringe of roof up at the sky, and he imagined the shock of her slipping off, tumbling down the rocky slope thirty yards to the path below. But she seemed sure of foot and---still leaning too far, he thought---cried out in mad enthusiasm, "The moon will rise now....I see light in the sky....did you see last night....or did you sleep too soon, tired from your trip?....I love the moon....she's ...who? Artemis...the hunter...huntress of men?....No....My mother told me never stare at full moon....can you think of that? I went crazy last night...I saw you come in the panga .....you were by yourself....I thought.... to come see you, but it was late....I didn't want to bother...you..." And her words went on in a staccato flurry, and she pulled away from the edge, dancing over to him and away again, in the glee he knew so well but could not show as freely as did she. Back to the brink swirling, leaning far over it, and he thought she was inclined too far, not so sure of foot, so he pushed out from his chair and scooted to the edge next her as if to glimpse the rising moon himself---which he knew was better seen from the kitchen patio---inclining his head, and using the same motion to grab her and ease her away from the black drop. She was breathing hard, muffling her laughter, trying to get free even as one hand gripped his elbow tightly. And it was his screaming blood that understood she was wonderful, snarling and wayward like a petulant cat pulled away from ripping the furniture. He did not let go, and she did not let go; illumination was seeping through chinks in the roof and would soon souse their brimming world. For a minute they grew quiet, just standing still, not looking at each other, taking the measure of their wishes. She melted a little, and he thought she might cry. Girlish or womanish? A gallant impulse prompted him to say, at last, "I thought of you, too, when the moon came up, wondering if you were here. I didn't see your light. But you're right, I was tired, and wanted just to wind down from my trip, alone." Of course, he did not mention the book he read for hours, much less his midnight walk to the jungle----what was the point? And she---what had she done when she "went crazy"? *Desolation Row* was playing now, and he recalled how flabbergasted he had been when he first heard it on the *Midnight Special* radio program. If it had seemed to solemnize a certain derangement, it was one he'd not been, or was too late to be, ready for in that post-Kerouac time. But the narcotic of the music stirred him anew, and he began a lively dance with her, acting out the romantic couple on a dance floor, abiding the oddly prophetic words Dylan twanged: *If you lean your head out far enough/ From Desolation Row.* But they were far from Desolation Row and, as they whirled about, a chalky slice of moon shot from the ridge of mountain and spilled to the floor a shaft of colorless light, a drained white suiting that goddess whose veil is never lifted.

"Where is your girlfriend?" she whispered in his ear. "We only live together when we are here," he dissembled, discerning a pretended jealousy in her question. In the same breath he drew her through the brightening spotlight and propelled her outside to the patio, where they trembled in the flood. Breaking apart, they sat on the low wall and watched tossing all about them the shadows of helpless palms in the wind---moondials, drunken and mocking. How many fraught minutes trickled down the hourglass as they sat close, savoring their tense hesitations, until he once more took her by the hand and drew her into the house, no longer the dance couple but lovers, to the nervous curtains that shielded the bedroom, and whipped them aside. A mosquito net was half open over the bed. At its edge, he waited to see what she would do, or, rather, waited to let her do it. One hand covered her mouth, yawing, and the other held his shirt, but he yanked away the one to taste her mouth while her clutching hand brought them down on the shuddering bed to tear off their clothes quickly. And it was no wonder that this had all been prefigured in the first glance of that morning. Moonlight soaked through the gauze, and the bed creaked on its ropes, swaying to the erotic rhythm of their appetites. *Feel it*, she murmured, *feeeel it.*

18

THE MOON NO LONGER cast a spotlight to the floor when they recovered, but had sailed well overhead; its light still swam zealous in their keep. The sheen of sweat on their bodies dried, and the coolness of the moon seemed to assuage their heat. Sprawled atop the sheets, their ruddy faces drained pale as they turned to each other, and each had its mask restored.

So it had been only a brief abandon---if that---for now she dragged a sheet over her body, as if it was not he who had devoutly possessed it. Or was it just customary female modesty, for her ardor had been unstinting, so the mien of shyness disguised perhaps everything but her pleasure? A mask might protect the heart from feared injury, but the soul---exposed or not--- should wear no mask. He thought that sex without love lost something, but sex with a pretense of it lost that much more. It was already a defeat to feign one feeling to gain another. If it was no more than appetite that had brought them to bed on this night, that deserved as much rejoicing as the tropical moon. Wasn't appetite rooted in the life force, an essential conduit for the duality of creation-destruction, love-hate? But the moon's languid though bright face shone with secondary light, and bestowed blessing or bewitchment merely impersonal---as an agent conducing the inscrutable. The score of incandescence blazed elsewhere.

He listened to the few birds muttering outside, as though restless in dreams, then got up to look out on the unfazed night from the kitchen. Becky spoke out from the sheets---perhaps a question--- so he grabbed a bottle from the fridge and rejoined her, offering a drink. She tipped the bottle roughly and handed it back, asking him what he would do. He revolved alternate answers in his head, not sure exactly what reference her question had. In the end, he said "nothing." He sat on the bed and stroked her leg through the sheet, making the bed sway again, and amusedly thought of the coordination needed for making love on a hanging bed. Sleeping on one with another was seemingly out of the question, but, of course, he had done it often. Becky was murmuring words from *Like a Rolling Stone,* and eased the bottle from his hands. He kissed her with beer still in her mouth, and she giggled, sputtering some on his chin, then unexpectedly threw off her sheet and sat up. "You're not a rolling stone, that's what I like about you," she burst out, and slid her hand up his back. "So I do gather moss," he said, ironically, wondering what he really meant, but went on anyway--- "You know what I see, revealed in the oblivion of passion?" He paused, perhaps to judge her gaze. "Something beyond personality, or prior to personality, like a simple connection with...." but struggled to find a different word to end his thought, having repressed the first one, which was "the cosmic." It was the consummate word to him, but words were alive and sensitive to misuse, easily spoiled---as that one was---by facile conversation. The body *is* a cosmos, as the atom is, as the planet is. He didn't finish the thought, but continued: "So the 'oblivion' of passion is really the oblivion of personality by quitting the daily mask, wiping away the layer that fends off the primordial." She looked at him quizzically, or appraisingly, and was slow to reply: "No....not a rolling stone, are you? My brother's head is all tangled up like yours, and I tell him he thinks too much. But so glad I am that you do more than think so much----ooh, more...I see you look at things.... the cat, my picture, anything....you're good to have." (She seeming not to know the connotation in English.) She scurried out past him, twirling from a hook the wrap she threw on, and flew to the bathroom. He heard the shower running, and the splash of water sounded so persuading he padded over and slipped in. It was cold, and they squirmed and clowned until they were shivering. She turned it off with a scream, and pulled two towels from a big basket hanging outside the door. "I make some coffee," she said, running to the kitchen, trailing the towel behind her. He looped the towel around his waist and went to the table where he thought the remains of the joint might be. Just the bag of pot was there, and a pack of Fiesta cigarettes. He lighted one, not much liking its taste, but smoked a little, watching as Becky made coffee by the sink soaked in moonlight. Rumi's line came to him:....."even the phrase 'each other' doesn't make any sense." Beyond notions of wrongdoing and rightdoing is a place where the world is too full to talk about, Rumi wrote. His own sympathy was securely there, and the sense he got, smoking the Fiesta and watching Becky's absorbed movements, was like that expansive feeling he'd had on the yacht years ago, mindless no doubt, amazed at the well being that rose to answer the smallest pleasure. Becky was singing remembered music from the Dylan tape, and she was clearly feeling good, with her own kind of rejoicing. As he watched her, in that moment he loved the woman she was, the woman she had been in bed, and the woman who could make so thoughtful a picture. So if the phrase "each other" made no sense, so what! The night made sense and he did not care about any other sense.

He crushed out the cigarette and shot to the kitchen, grasping her as she was pouring two cups of coffee. "What are you doing," she protested without protest. "Let's drink it outside, on the patio," he said, and they went and sat in the same spot as before. The hotel lights were off, and there were none to be seen in the village. There was only the moon, high overhead, and fitful shards of moonlight glinting from thousands of palms, which had all virtually lost their moondial shadows. The night was vast and naked and they were near naked in it. Everything was just as naked in it as the moon; it was as if the veil of the goddess *had* been lifted. Punctual sounds of waves regaling the rocky shore rose up the slope. The birds were asleep, the bats were asleep, even the insects were meek. But their hearts were awake, beating together, and cherished a mirth that hummed along with the coffee. The bay reflected a deep, white, soundless gong of brilliance, tearing at their hearts without tempering the scamper of mirth. Their smallness solitary in such largeness seemed almost not credible to him, *preternatural.* Anomalous word, that, but he could think of none better, for the world around him *was* immense and stupefying, and he *was* there for it, stunned and unshielded in boundless moonbeams, an illumination that unveiled as if to anoint even the farthest miles of the unpeopled Pacific spreading beyond their cove.

Becky prattled on about plans for tomorrow; made fun of one or another village character; said she'd given five pesos to Agripina, the cheerful lady beggar, on the beach; joked about her sketch subject. Sensibly, he listened while their cups were sipped empty, until with a sigh she grew calm in her posture, as if suddenly lonesome. Rejoicing was done and he could hear coming out of quiet the sifting lapse of time. Wordlessly they returned to the bed, ceding the night to Morpheus after a final flourish of caresses. He slumbered soundly and did not know if the bed swayed.

19

He awoke before day, and found his senses still vexed by the singe of amorous fervency---but he relished the trouble. Higher on the slope, the damp chill of spindrift at dawn did not reach her panoplied bed as it did his; he lay there not huddled but becalmed. Through the slats that walled the alcove he saw splayed in the sky a milky glow from the moon that had fallen below a silhouetted ridge curved as a cutlass.

The sound of birds stirring mingled with distant splashes of swells on the rocks below. He stayed quietly for long minutes to delight in being laved by the shimmer of light drizzling through the gauze---and cleave to the pleasure of waking in a sleeping woman's warmed and scented bed. When he eased himself out through the mosquito net, Becky raised her head for a moment, but fell back. He dressed, scratching inflamed *jejene* bites: it would take a week or more to get inured to them. Where was the flashlight? But he hardly needed it; the world outside was illumined in silver outline. He thought of leaving a note, and grappled with banal words in his head, but dismissed them all. Then he saw a sheet of paper lying on the floor and picked it up and looked for a pencil or pen. He found only crayons on the

small table, so took one and drew two figures on the paper---
kindergarten stick figures really---which were in chartreuse, and
under them he scribbled their two names; above, the word "yes".
He put the sheet by the sink, under a coffee cup, and noticed the
datura bells drooping in a glass. He had forgotten them, but they
looked as if they had made an effort to blare up and failed. On
the patio he saw opposite the mountain the yellow glimmer of
dawn, and went down the stepping stones to the flat outcrop by
the gate. A dog loped by on the path to the village without the
slightest halt in its motion, as if it were late for an appointment.
The hut of Silent Jack was to his left, and he heard sounds coming
from it. Jack would soon be gathering up the gear for a diving
trip with a trio of village brothers, their livelihood earned by
spear fishing. To the right was his house, looking stooped under
the parota tree, and with the faint gleam of the lamps he had left
burning it was welcoming. He climbed the boulder steps to the
back gate, and went in. Once inside, it seemed dank and spiritless,
so he turned up the lamps, but he was at a loss. Empty of affect,
the vacancy of the house oppressed him. Should he have stayed
with Becky after all? No, he trusted his timing, and knew she
would have her own plans. She had said as much in their last
talk on the patio. He would find himself again, and better soon.
He sat down at the table and read more pages of The Magus, but
it could not hold him. He got up to make coffee. It was getting
light outside, the light of violent life, and the moon had lost all its
dominion. Motors were starting up, and the village was coming
to that life in the same pattern as the day before, a pattern that
could not be vitiated by repetition any more than breathing could.
And though it was a routine, were not these villagers all about
to embrace a day of uncertain outcome? A day with a certain
outcome might be imagined or desired, but with what reliance?
Until the foreigners came with their dollars there was hardly even
the idea of outcome. The propensity to believe in certain outcomes
perhaps did not help create them, and he thought of pages in
Hume he'd read years before. To examine such habits of the mind

was irresistible, and with some strange logic led to nostalgia for the past. No, it was more than nostalgia. Recollections of the past were often more compelling than any fiction, which, at the same time, they resembled. He marveled at those whose memory seemed unfailing. His own presented the incidents he selected with a lapidary finish, all roughness and accident polished out, and pinging with a satisfying emotional tone. True, some of the things he searched for in his past turned out to be different than those lapidary versions---like his childhood had---so perhaps exact memory was not completely absent in him. But if truth was stranger than fiction, it was because 'truth' is often bad fiction and in dire need of reworking. He had the hope---or trust---that what memory failed to discover, imagination would. *Imagination*, not *invention*. Descriptive power might joyfully do some justice to the night's beauty, but there was little point in trying to explain it. Grace retreats disconsolate even from trim expositions. What he had thought paused on the steps going up to Becky's house was right: we strive towards the most artful, most exquisite, expression precisely to sweeten the bitterness of our incomprehension, the bitterness of not speaking in the voice but only in the guise of gods.

20

WHILE HE STOOD IN the kitchen dazed by this train of thought---
was it inspired or deceived?---he heard the coffee boil over. He
poured the dregs into the little green *jarra*, rinsed and refilled
the pot impatient to replenish the cup, and finally sat down
at the table, hoping to rearrange his musings into a coherent
order. Still the train did not stop but puffed into a new landscape
as he contemplated the table and the chairs around it. They
were a set of *equipal*, made from palm strips, twigs, and wood
covered in pigskin, a design subsisting from deep in the past of
the indigenous people. They had sat on the floor for many years,
and the table had to be maneuvered into a stable position on the
original, unevenly seated cobblestones. No one gave it a thought
at the time for the delight in just being there. But after some
years, he had the cobbles cemented over by Ramon with a creamy
white compound that gave it a look of marble. The counters in
the kitchen were finished similarly, but with a rose tint in the
mixture. Now the chairs and table were positioned with ease, but
remained the same *tipico* furniture, center of waking life, whether
it was he who sat around or strangers. So if he wanted coherent
order in his thoughts, why not be done with metaphysics and

begin a consideration of events and happenings in which the table figured? But where to start, where to end? Was this one of those attractive plans that fizzled out when something else grabbed attention? There was precious ore in the deeps of memory, but its patient extraction might be tedious, or improbable. More likely, it was better to let things surface in their own time, even given how chancy that might be.

As he stared out the window to the garden, balancing the cup of sludgy coffee in distraction, sure enough, an image surfaced: he and his wife were sitting at the table with Carla, the woman who had built the house that Becky now lived in, and they were drinking coffee in the morning, while Nico and Carla's little girl, Crystal, were playing outside. They were passing the first joint of morning around when they saw the immigration officials coming through the front gate, striding brisk. With stunning presence of mind, Carla, in one seamless movement, pinched out the joint and stuffed it into her bra in seconds. It was amazing that Juan Pena, the chief, smelled nothing as he barged in, with a big laugh but ominous manner. They rifled the ashtray, finding only cigarette butts, then rummaged through the house. Where was their stash, he wondered? Still under rocks in a can; Carla had brought the joint. Juan spoke pretty good English, so they all bantered for a while and Juan flirted with Carla, until finally the cohort left with obvious disappointment to go out to the Point, where there was a kind of hostel run by a California woman. Now they breathed easier, insouciantly relighting the joint: the prey had outwitted their hunters. Half an hour later a line of ten or fifteen young gringos marched down the path in front of the house, prisoners led by the officers who were laughing in triumph, having toted up an ample score. They had all been busted, and were later deported. A roach had been found in an ashtray in their house, sufficient to make one and all guilty....seeing them, Carla gushed with the garish jollity of Las Vegas, where she worked as a croupier, and life went on......A nugget from the mine below.....however small....

In his mood of near lethargy, it seemed as though he could sit there all day flipping through the files of memory. But that inclination was definitely passing as the day brightened. A surge of voices and clamoring sea birds crowded the morning, and the sun topping the village turned the bay into the usual mirror of blinding bursts. The chill in the house dissipated in the new heat, and the heat brought hunger. There was nothing but eggs and the tin of sardines and a few vegetables. The beans were swollen and split in the pot; he filled it with fresh water, threw in some crushed garlic, and set it under a flame. He had to search for the opener, but once the sardines were out Tao appeared from somewhere and he put a chunk on the floor for her. How did she know? He rarely fed her from a can because he rarely opened one. But he was not her sole benefactor. She made the rounds of houses, to Becky or Martita, and to Rasa in the house below, where Santos the fisherman used to live with his numerous children. Now it was rented to her, while Santos lived in a small house he had built up the hill. Where was Rasa? He had heard nothing coming from her house. She, the mindful elder, a composed woman who lived alone and was cherished as a cynosure by many. A pot of coffee was always steaming on her stove.

He finished breakfast and sprawled in the hammock. The weave of the palapa roof drew a delighted attention from him, following the undulations and off-weaves from one end to another, caused by the irregularity of the fronds and the haphazard diligence of the workers. It seemed to him as if each pole, crossbeam and zone had its own quirk of personality, but the sum of their imperfections remarkably added up to a handsome perfection.

21

H<small>E SMOKED ONE OF</small> his Delicados, and launched the hammock in flight by nudging the floor with a foot. He thought of his night with Becky. They'd known each other a few years without connecting. It was not quite true that, as she'd said, he was always with another. Sometimes *she* was with another. If it had been neither seduction nor conquest, it was more than a fling and less than an affair. Their game had no frills, just the authenticity of biology, and was here in the jungle entirely accordant. *Gaudeamus igitur*, for life one day will seem painfully short, and the earth will have us. They both knew what they were doing, and there would be no question of commitment, even for the while. She would not *appropriate* his time here, but share some. She felt the same way, he reassured himself. Stretched out diagonal, he was almost as flat as in bed, and from it he could see into the *topanco*, a narrow second story made possible by the higher roof, but completely open at this end, and taking up half the length of the house. Except for storage, it was unused, but he would make a bedroom of it in the summer for Nico. A crude ladder leaned against the viga supporting the open end, and he got out of the hammock and climbed up to peer in. The other end was partly open under the roof, so the topanco was well ventilated. He had also cut out a pair of sections a meter square in the roof, which were replaced with plastic sheets, for light.

He would go out, he decided, and without any plan in mind he showered and dressed in fresh clothes. Not the beach, this time, he thought, and put on pants and shirt, refilling the net bag with usual stuff. He remembered to turn off the beans, not yet finished. There were only two directions he could go: left to the Point, where there were more gringo houses; right to the village and beyond, with several forks. His feet took him right, through the elephant ears and the carpet of stubborn creeper, which seemed greener from the water he'd splashed briefly around the day before. At the gate he glanced for a moment at the path which wound above Becky's house and on to others higher up the hill, past the white castle of Pipeline Jim, skirting the village cemetery with its tiny plastic crosses, and up into the mountains to Chacala. It was an arduous climb of three or four hours, and he had done it once a few years ago challenged by Jimmy, a visiting old friend from another life, an intrepid hiker. The trail was one trampled out by horse and mule, and even above the palm line marl and scree persisted. Taunting parrots screeched, and sandy gray birds scuttled, twee-ing in the bracken. Gray, the color of nondescript, the color of obliteration, of the nearly invisible. He had to stop and rest frequently. When they arrived in the rustic town of scruffy wooden houses and dusty streets forsaken past noon he was dripping with sweat and exhausted, while Jimmy shrugged off the travail with a sneer. Their reward came in finding a cheerful *abuela* who guessed their need and beckoned them to her house for an *almuerzo*, which seemed incredibly sumptuous though it consisted of no more than the staple corn and beans and chile of the Mexican peasant anywhere. There were a few shreds of meat and cabbage, but it was the tortillas that he held fondest, fresh made and hot from the *comal* with heavenly taste. They rested after lunch in tattered hammocks, and the *dona* brought them boiled coffee with cinnamon. This charged him with renewed vigor for the return, which at first was much easier, but then became more dangerous, as the descent seemed even steeper than the climb; slipping or twisting an ankle was a constant hazard. It was late afternoon before they caught their first glimpse of the bay, and the sight was encouraging. But the last few hundred yards of the way were the most treacherous, and as they were inching along, two village boys came running down, shouting in youthful glee, and flashed by them barefoot, trailing an echo. The effect was stunning, and he felt inspired. He tightened his sandals and strode down steeled with assurance, ignoring the sliding, and marched into the house ahead of Jimmy, where Donna was working in the kitchen. He wasted no time in slugging down shots of raicilla from the bottle he had brought back, turning his already rubbery legs into putty.....another nugget from below....

He went on to the village, but lingered again by the datura plant in the gully. Had the cut flower opened in the night and closed by the time he got up, like these? Or did it yawn in full-moon-light, heavy with final sleep? He shrugged off the curiosity, but for some reason it nagged at him, as if premonitory of a shunned task. Datura was jimson weed, a strange and possibly dangerous psychedelic; he'd never taken it---could that be the reason?

Horses were tethered in front of Martin's house, the ones that would soon be going to the beach. Here, a path led to the waterfall behind the village, going from Eva's beer hut to track the creek. Ten minutes into the jungle, he came to it, eighty or a hundred feet high. It dropped sheer to a swirling pool, large and shallow enough for children to play in. A hut off to the side sold cold drinks and coconuts. He bought a coconut, and watched the man chop it open on a block and put a straw in the hole. He drained it in a guzzle, and thought of the 'green nuts' of Trinidad, offered from the back of a flat bed truck by a youth standing free, wielding with fortunate precision his machete, without a block. There, after drinking the sweet milk, the nut was halved and a spoon cut from one side with two smart flicks of the machete, to savor the jelly.

Here, the meat was hard and he ate little. That West Indian sound of *green nut, mahn* stayed in his mind while he pondered the jungle from his stool of coconut trunk. Spray from the cascade cooled the air, and rainbows shimmered out in delight from the explosion at the bottom. The illusion of slowed motion in the water's leap, like a forgiveness of gravity, was impressive. A whisper would not be heard here. He listened to the rhythm of the fall, distinct in a pulsating current, as though it had the inflection of droning speech. The strength of the water, its will-----and such he now believed it had!-----patiently concealed a purpose, for the understanding of which it seemed to be asking. But what was there to understand? Water falling over a ledge to a pool below. Beautiful, but without meaning. Yet it appeared to him more poignant with meaning than almost anything else. Were thoughts altered or obscured by the effort to put them in words? *When a word reaches far as the lips the mind can no longer pronounce it.* Was this an apostasy? But *language doesn't have any sense,* Rumi said---yet he sang in it for meaning anyway. Why else write volumes of poetry? The gurus who said *just do it* nevertheless filled shelves with their books! And if he had once thought that writing ten great lines would justify his life, none were needed to justify the waterfall, or the morning.

He got up from the stool, and realized that his intention had all along been to go *above* the waterfall, where there were no houses, perhaps no people. There was a trail, almost hidden, thirty yards behind the soft drink hut. From there it rose innocently into the hills, but soon doubled back and went up precipitously to a place about ten yards over a deep pool, where the water swirled peacefully just before its plunge. He edged toward it, not wanting to be seen, as if it were forbidden, and quietly faded into the hill. With the anticipation of an illicit thrill, he made his way up, as he had many times over the years. He could not remember how he had first discovered the way. On the hardened ground he climbed over rock outcroppings and tangled tree roots until he finally stood above the pool. Now the trail grew faint, following the little river up the mountain, and it was evident that other feet had walked it.

Oh, it was tantalizing, that pool! But he continued up the riverbank until he was out of earshot of the fall, merely a hundred yards. Now there was just the gurgling sound of a brook, overhung with thick branches of tangled trees and shrubs, through which dappled sunlight filtered. Diminutive birds twittered furtively in the shadows, nervous with his presence. A serene wildness pervaded the place, not much like the river scene of the day before because almost totally removed from human influence. It might have been miles away from the village; not even the bay could be seen. There was no vast sky there. Vines draped themselves around whatever they found, and hung down from the highest branches. Bromeliads and orchids bloomed shyly in the elbows of limbs. The accidents of lodged debris or stones created marvelous little pools, some brilliant, some stagnant, where another kind of life lived and died, the caprice of nature all in a cubic foot of water, while inches away the creek rushed by. He sat on a large rock in the shade and studied one of these eddies, losing himself in the tiny destinies playing out. Then he stretched out on another, a granite slab, in the sun, to warm himself and to watch the glide of dragonflies and float of butterflies. A wasp zoomed around. A big iguana entered his eye when it turned its head on a branch ten feet away. "…..*in wildness is the preservation of the world…*" Thoreau famously wrote. And the world that was preserved in the glen, in the river scene, and the entire mountain, gave no hint of ceasing, nor was it deviated by any threat of encroachment from its truth. It felt like he was on a stage where no players strode or declaimed, whose largeness was not measured by fortune or misfortune. As large as it was, and as small as he was, nothing got excluded: "*We could see how ample and roomy is nature.*" Thoreau wrote about one of his walks. There was a sense of endless distance and time that dwelled unconfounded. It was not glee that he felt, but joy. And he wished that he had brought a bamboo flute with him, as he used to, to sing his brimming love through it. The cane itself grew music mute within, but only through breath were songs transported to release.

22

No vista or pageant of grandeur affected him more than the scene in which he lolled. He was startled by the attention it demanded, and saw an intimate corner of the world where enchantment shimmered in proper scope. It equaled the emotional scale of another place, the sylphid woods of the Indiana Dunes, where he had rambled in the summers of young adolescence. He was not yet old enough to mourn for that lost youth, but it emerged anyway, blurred as if by tears. In each place there was the same lonely beauty--- blinding, hurtful, baffling. Choked with both joy and the fruitless impotence of words, he was taken by a breath-giving astonishment, and whistled *Sheep may safely graze*, simulating the absent flute that turned breath into music. 'Singing in the wilderness', like Omar, but without wine, without a *thou*. If he sang in the wilderness no one would hear. An hour passed, or two.

He tripped down to the pool above the fall, and sat on the camber of smooth rock that rimmed it, in full sun. Even on this promontory in the canyon, only a slip of the bay was seen, and no beach. The water slid over the lip of the ancient basin and fell innocent, only a quiet echo resounding from below. He took off his clothes and dove into the water. It was cold and tonic, shocking his heart. Twenty-five feet across and surrounded by polished boulders, he could not touch its bottom, but tread in place against the current for a few minutes, facing heedless away from the fall. He crawled back onto the boulder, stretched naked on the warm stone, feeling sensual, excited. Warming on his back he saw a bird gliding far up, in a window between the mountains, circling as if dozing on the air, a frigate bird. Then there were two, three. From a crevice in the wall thirty feet away came the sound of squabbling------birds or squirrels? Time was told in heartbeats, and when he turned over on his stomach he could count them clearly over the blood surging in his groin.....*into a perfect work time does not enter.*....said Thoreau. This truth was never in doubt: life was worth living only as its worth was lived. His body was dry and strong; half an hour drowsed by before he dressed to forestall the certain burn. He smoked a cigarette halfway, threw it into the pool and watched as it seemed to deliberate before making its way over the edge. He was reluctant to leave; hours were counted for nothing. He drank a little water from his scooping hands, and noticed the lead water pipes branching off in several directions. Almost every year another affluent resident put in a new pipe at a higher intake than the others, and he saw tribal wars prefigured in so harmless a hint of conflict. Man's dominion over nature was dire, foreboding, fated---possibly commanded. *Give me a wildness whose glance no civilization can endure,* wrote Thoreau. But even he had lived at Walden merely two years, and was a townsman.

The water he drank made him hungry and, in spite of himself, suggested a return to the village. It was only a fifteen minute walk back, but it would seem like a long journey. In his bag was a banana, and he ate it: it was not enough, so he soon put on his sandals and made his way up the slippery boulder back to the trail. On the way down, he avoided a particular, thick root almost buried in an unlikely niche where once, haplessly barefoot, he had ripped out a toenail. The nail grew back, distorted, a rueful souvenir; now he was mindful going down. When he emerged by the soft drink hut he reminded himself, now that the paradise of the river would be replaced by the purgatory of the village, to hold fast to that sense he carried of having been startled up from a drowse. He felt a disappointment that was fortunately temporary. On the trail from the waterfall to the village were plastic wrappers, cans and bottles discarded by the uncaring. The villagers themselves were careless with garbage, and now that modern materials were replacing simpler ones, the refuse might remain for quite a while; even a pig will not eat plastic. The tremulous feeling holding him in thrall to the spotless scene he had just left would quickly change, and a larger forbearance of the village life prevail: *Such a day is a truce to vice*---again Thoreau--- and in ten minutes the vice would look like virtue, the travesty of heedlessness become the comforts of home.   He reached the ramada where Eva sat, chatting with another woman. She looked up at him long enough to chuckle her "Coca Cola nada mas" jingle, and he stopped at a few tiendas to replenish provisions, before going down the path to his house. There was the drooping datura, and he thought again of the blooms in the glass. And perhaps he would call up to Becky; they had made no plan to reunite. But just as he got near his gate, he looked across the tangled lot that fronted Rasa's house, and saw a figure moving inside. He went in, sidestepping the debris of the coconut palms---which Santos still harvested---to her open doorway, and there she was, standing at the stove. She turned to meet his gaze, and on her face a slow grin tinged with customary irony widened to a chipper smile.

23

He stepped over the threshold into a vaulted but spare interior, and gave her an eager hug. The house seemed larger than Becky's, cool and bright, and faced the bay behind a stone retaining wall barricading it from the waves.

He wondered where she'd been. The ironic grin reappeared as she shrugged around to the stove and grumbled, "Huh! I was in Vallarta. Luv is moving out here; he says he won't put up with the *scene* there anymore. I just thought I could help a little," she replied with playful exasperation. "Luv" was the name Alfonso de la Vega had assumed, at the same time he'd exchanged hip Vallarta costume for the austere cotton of the New Age. It was probable even that name was a *nom de guerre*, for he had come down from provincial Culiacan, becoming in Vallarta a big artist and designer, center of a gay coterie that enlivened things there. "He's taken the *rancho* that Benino doesn't use, and a small entourage is coming with him. Nahoo and Parko and I don't know who else," she continued, now with searing impatience. "I suppose it *will* be good, but they have to make such a drama out of it, it drives me up the wall. And there's Nahoo whining all the time, 'What will I do without a fan in my bedroom, how can I stand all the *bugs*, how will I see all my friends?' And so on and on. Luv tries to calm him down, and tells him it's for his own good…then Nahoo shuts up like a chastised boy, and curls up at his feet. He's used to being the celebrity, the envied chic restaurant owner, and now he's a *follower*…it's hard on him." With a sigh she recovered herself, and laughed. "Oh, I'll get through it, but what a *trip* it is," and 'trip' was a favored word threaded into her talk.

He remembered Nahoo from the restaurant, cool vanguard in the resort town, when his name was Craig. Apparently, with Gandhian garb came an Indic name. *Her* name was adopted as well---and though Luv insisted it be Ratsa, he did not like or accept *that* change.

"Want some coffee?" she prompted.

"Sure," he replied, and followed her around like a puppy as she puttered. Rasa seldom went out, and was usually *a la casa* to many gringos who stayed in the village. There were always the latest volumes on 'higher consciousness' lying around, and weighty discussion could go on to late hours, stoked by coffee and marijuana---but not alcohol. This was where he'd met Joe and Martita first, three or four years before.

A large, square coffee table occupied the center of the room, with cushions strewn around, and they settled there. She inquired about his wife and son, but was soon relating the news closer at hand. Rasa could lend authority to any gossip, as if the smallest foible apprised a *cosmic* significance---a word *she* was not reluctant to use. She went on about the tribulations of Luv's arrival with his retinue. Luv now laid claim to the status of initiated *guru*, and she considered herself a somewhat leery adherent, because she did not believe in his 'sainthood', only in his abilities, his power. She could not totally dismiss anything that made a claim on 'higher consciousness'---- she had patience for everything but outright nonsense, and would confront without fail those who uttered it---- even when that claim was possibly phony. She gave it the benefit of the doubt. But once the motive was clear, or the pretense exposed, her judgment was cynical, her words forceful.

She had traveled with Luv, and was witness to his insight, but was also aware of the mind games he liked to play. Luv might be a bit of Gurdjieff, but he was also a bit of Crowley, and liked to work his 'magic' unopposed. She kept an open mind, but the melodrama of the 'scene' was obviously not to her taste. She preferred the dramas of couples that shifted in faux Shakespeare fashion, mostly the male and the female---not anything he would gainsay.

As they sipped coffee, he felt an altered brightness in the day; yes, like *a truce to vice*. The bay outside was nearly eye level, and the bursts of sunlight stippled in the waves were less sharp than from his higher vantage. Rasa encouraged a calm but pungent comfort in her space. Yesterday he'd ached for 'reflection or corroboration'; now here they were, induced by her offhand, allowing him to understand their tarrying ache quenched by the privilege of being alone with her---keen comrades in a sympathy truer than consolation.

The subject of Luv was dismissed by a wave of her hand, and with endearing focus she now picked up a thick volume of Sri Aurobindo, a name she pronounced simply, "Aborindo", and said, "There's a lot of *information* in this book", and opened it immediately to read a passage:

> The divine existence is of the nature not only of freedom, but of purity, beatitude and perfection.....The divinising of the normal material life of man and of his great secular attempt of mental and moral self-culture in the individual and the race by this integralisation of a widely perfect spritual existence would thus be the crown alike of our individual and of our common effort.......worthy of those whose dedicated vision perceives that God dwells concealed in humanity.

She read in a clear voice, without emphasis, though looking directly at him every few words, as if to make sure he registered their import. Her manner lacked didacticism as much as it lacked sentimentality, and her alert, wrinkled features commanded attention, assumed it. She herself seemed always awake, day or night, to minister and enlighten. She did not talk about her past, and details of her present, personal life was not a subject that interested her; she said she no longer lived a personal life.

Putting the book down on the table, she began a telling analysis of the larger political situation, post Vietnam, relating it to the passage she had just read, as well as to other ideas in the book. He could not imagine where she found time to read all these books, but then, time was no luxury in the village---certainly not to one with so little personal life to undergo---and he thought that probably no tome was too abstruse for her to ignore.

She got up to check a pot of beans cooking on the stove, and to refresh their coffee. Returning with the cups, she said, "Becky has been coming in a lot, and we've had some good talks. She's been getting out more, not keeping to herself so much, a lot more straightened out. Have you seen her?" But before he could answer, a woman came through the door with a laughing, southern-sounding greeting, and clapped her hands when she saw him sitting by the low table. It was Kristan, Melman's old girlfriend; they hugged and their recent night together was left unacknowledged. She was only a few days back from Houston, where she had been working with a Chinese health practitioner who had some novel techniques for treating illness, and she was flushed in talking of them.

24

"THE MAIN IDEA BEHIND his method is called *solar nutrition*. You start the morning eating foods that grow high up in early sun, and move to lower ones during the day until night, when you eat foods that grow below ground or in the dark. Of course, there's more to it than that, and it gets complicated, but that's the basic idea. He also runs a clinic where high colonics are given." Kristan paused to watch the effect her words were having, and did not have to wait long for Rasa to announce how fine she thought the idea was, but that it might be difficult to give up late coffee drinking since, surely, it was only proper for day. And her remark seemed timed for that moment, as she poured out a cup of it for Kristan, who, if she noticed the irony, ignored it, though insisting that the method was not inflexible. Besides, there were coffees that grew *lower to the ground* than some, and could be drunk in the afternoon. And night, he wondered?

Even so, he reflected that the cunning elegance of such a *timed* schedule was admirable, and he'd once been attracted to the *macrobiotic* scheme, just because of its simplicity. But all these seemed no more than notions in the head, and could not for long rival the lure of good food eaten whenever the sensuous appetite chose it. But he said nothing, preferring to listen to Rasa and Kristan carry the conversation, from which he gradually withdrew his attention. A breeze was blowing through the house, and the bay was losing its sparkle; the yacht was pulling anchor, the mainsail flapping in readiness for a good breeze, a good tack. Where would it go? If the journey was more important than the destination, he thought, that was because we own the journey, whereas the destination owns us. He was no longer sure what the two women were talking about, and fell into his accustomed reverie. He would follow casual conversation for only so long; to disguise his sudden disinterest he got up and went toward the retaining wall by the water as if to observe something there. The people on the yacht were yanking ropes, and he could hear their voices but the wind blew away the words. The boy was in the stern, hands on the wheel. Even as he watched, the lush swirl of the pool above the waterfall came into his mind. Nurturing a saved sense of ownership, he evoked the heat of the boulder beside the cold pool that filled and depleted continuous, in the same moment. The day was moving in that simple time, and the quietude of this rhythm was instilled in everything. Past the yacht and the bay, his eyes swept the beach and saw that it was empty: the boats had gone, the canoes hauled back up to rest, the strand clean. He had been long above the waterfall, and conscious only of his own rhythm: *exiled by temperament......*

And was *his* journey like a journey of exile? A lone wolf traveling secret trails, enthralled in its hunger, yet desperate to make out the obscure origin of such a strangeness. Not by choice self absorbed, perhaps only by habit. He was not entirely uncomfortable with this habit, but could be embarrassed by his lolling tongue, the wolf panting, ready to pounce if cornered. With an instant, shocking clarity, he remembered the summer beach cottage, set on blocks, in the Dunes when he was a boy. The wind often twisted fissures in the sand beneath it, hollowing out defiles like tiny caves. He would hide in them and watch his cousins playing outside, feeling safe, free and intact. If his mother called, he could emerge as if from some boyish adventure, knowing how he'd feel exonerated by relieving her concern at not seeing him. Now he wonders, Forgiven of what? Of leaving the womb? For some other---the cave? Rather a Freudian parse, what! True, he let no childhood punishment reach him deeply enough to matter. Still, in the midst of any crowd he could hide alone, savoring it. His shoulders hunched into the impermeable as he grew up, so the lone wolf finally trotted the trails with no alibi proffered.

These images brought a certain discomfort as he stared out into the last of the bright day, and he was aware again of the women talking, still settled on the cushions. There was earnestness in Kristan's voice, and Rasa was speaking to her in steady encouragement. He walked back to the kitchen and sniffed the simmering pot of beans. He remembered being hungry, that he had not finished cooking his own beans, but no impulse came. With his thoughts had come a suspension of time, even of this *drop-by-drop* kind of time, and all the short fingers of shadows outside made sundials without numbers; even so, time 'not worth measuring' was somehow being measured. And it was being measured without his permission---despite that suspension. What could be done about it? Fill it with something. The shadows were hardly wavering as he looked, but he thought they would if he looked away. The illusion of outstaring time...of outlasting it.

The garlic fragrance of the beans teased his appetite, and this time presumed a decision. "Are the beans done?" he asked. Rasa shrugged her shoulders, so he found a spoon to taste them. "What do you think?" she laughed. "Still a little crunchy," he said, a test his hunger ignored. Kristan was smiling weakly from her cushion, so he knew she'd been interrupted in some confession. "I could go to town and get some tortillas; they might be done when I got back," he offered. "Good idea....why don't you?... I guess you're hungry," she teased.

So he bowed a gesture to the seated women, and made his way out to the path, through the sea of fascinating shadows doddering in the breeze. The sun was tilting down in the west, and it would soon go behind the mountain he and Jerry had scaled in their foray to Chacala. The gully with the datura lay just beyond Rasa's gate, and he paused there again, invoking the spirit that dwelled----or hovered---in it. It was a spirit with vagrant moods, and the mood now partook of the somnolence that seeps into late afternoon......*A tiny creek trickles its way past a brick cottage, into a muddy thicket overgrown with shrubs and small trees, then disappears into the bay through a hole in a crumbling retaining wall......* If the language describing it was inadequate, that spirit was palpable without a definite *belief* in it---beliefs were sticky, adverse. Walking by the gully never failed to evoke peculiar alterations of atmosphere or attention: fluttering eyelids, shivering spine, even wrinkled nose. This was far different from the glen above the waterfall, because the effect was largely man made, the result almost of accident. The spirit seemed both enchanted and afflicted, beyond caring if the words whispered out were symbolic...... *When a word reaches as far as the lips, the mind can no longer pronounce it.* So had Reason long tricked him. Thick tomes of philosophy were laid waste in this understanding, but it was an understanding challenged anew in every awakening. When you fell out of bed you fell right into the habit of mistaking the word for the thing, the map for the trip, or the menu for the meal. The mind counts on being tricked. It was on the horns of a dilemma that life was spent, and awareness was pricked out at the tip of an acicula. Nails kept Senor Christ on the Cross. Bristling spikes or stipes grew freely in the gully, as the jungle would quickly take back anything left unattended. The spirit persisted, happy in gloom, while some unaccountable portent impended, as if other revenant spirits abounded in hiding; to a ghost another ghost is solid.

He found the *tortilleria* closed, but was able to get chuckling Eva to give him half a kilo for a few pesos. With a grin, she pointed to Sarita, like a procurer. He bought a fat avocado in another store, and returned to Rasa's hearth with only a hurried glance down the gully. The tortillas, still warm in their paper wrap, had tortured his appetite--- he ate a couple on the trail.

As he came in, Rasa and Kristan were now solemnly engaged at the table throwing coins for the I Ching. Kristan was counting heads and tails, lines broken and solid, constructing the hexagram. He dropped the tortillas on the kitchen counter and put on the stove a griddle to reheat them. A basket nearby had some chiles and onions in it, so he chopped them up and asked if there was a tomato anywhere. Rasa said she was out, so he quickly ran up to his house to get one. When he returned, Kristan was reading from the book her thrown fortune. It was 46, named Advancement, and she was delighted with its message: "The coming success is tremendous in scope since the foundation it rests upon has been developed with true devotion" and has "a timely accord with the tendencies of the cosmos." As she continued reading the fortune, he finished making the crude salsa and, piling some beans onto a warm tortilla, added a spoonful on and rolled it up. Did they want some? Not yet, they replied, so he made up a couple more and put them on a plate with slices of avocado and proceeded avidly to eat them. He wondered how this meal fit into the scheme of solar nutrition, and realized that it wouldn't. The avocado was for morning while the onion was for night. Only the beans and tortilla were for afternoon, and he was not sure where the chile fit in. Had it grown close to the ground in a bush or high in a tree? Did any chiles grow high in a tree? He did not know, but knew that right now he did not care. He was entirely given over to hunger and its appeasement. The mindless body surrendering without a fight to satisfy sheer appetite. The question of appetite again. No problema. There was no one to apologize to, unless it was the rapt women hunched over the table, pondering the words of the oracle. But they could not care less, as they saying went. He ate, just standing up in the kitchen, and mused as he watched the shadows outside, fading without a sigh in the falling light. And while they pondered words from a book, he thought he was immersed in a kind of oblivion far from theirs, but one into which they would soon go, as did all animals.

The plate was empty, the food gone. And with it went the oblivion. He looked around, almost like an expectant dog. The empty plate seemed comical. There was nothing to do but reenter the conversation.

25

BUT JUST AS HE was about to, Rasa got up and came into the kitchen. "How were the beans? Done?" "A bit more cooking wouldn't hurt," he said, "but they tasted good to me."

"Time for a joint," she said, and reached under the counter to retrieve a small jar of pot. "Kristan got a good reading. Want to throw it yourself?" The question was lathered with humor, and it was clear that Rasa thought it a fine thing to do, if rather superfluous. If you were receptive----one of the hexagrams is called The Receptive----anything you came up with was instructive, hopefully oracular. The array of 64 situations described in the ancient book appeared integral, cyclic as earth and sky, and ignored theism---unlike the Bible, or any other 'religious' text. But there were some who could hardly make a move without consulting it: Rasa once related how Nahoo would not take even a shower unless he first threw the coins. What could possibly be said about that? "There's nothing I want to ask at the moment," he asserted; "today, everything is perfectly clear." He looked up to see if she caught his irony, but she had gone back to the table to roll the joint, and said nothing. Kristan was motionless there, absorbed in re-reading the pages of her thrown hexagram. He looked at her carefully from across the room, with the empty plate still in his hand. She was a strongly built woman, with long, tangled brown hair, tough hands, and a determined manner. She had found something, cleaving to it tightly, and would not let go. And why should she, he thought. From being the effect of someone else's cause, the willful Melman, she now owned herself through this dedication. The pliancy she'd had that night she came to him for succor and solace was gone; in its place a discovered bravery. Never mind that it was the bravery of doctrine. A chunk of driftwood in the sea, to which any drowning man will cling. Her concentration on the message was touching, and he was suddenly in deep sympathy with her. While Rasa rolled the joint, she spoke in a soothing tone to her, as if to one languishing in illness. Kristan looked up from the page, with an expression of wonder or bliss shining on her face. "Just amazing," she breathed.

The light was receding quickly, *as if from a dimmer* he thought again. Tonight the moon would be late, and the lack of a plan did not discourage him. Outside, the shadows had dissolved into pools of grayness; though the sun was low behind the mountain, it had not set. He slid the plate into the sink, finally. He relished this tentativeness while snared by Kristan's enthusiasm. She was going on about the methods she hoped to learn in the clinic of her Chinese healer, whose name was Adano, and how she would apply his teaching to her work in the village. There was no doctor here, only midwives and herbalists----Santiago was one----and she thought she was needed. To behold such earnestness tweaked his sympathy, and he went over to Kristan and told her how glad he was to see her happy. This was no lie, and he curried no favor. Rasa had fired up the joint and passed it to him. He took a drag and sat down on one of the cushions as Kristan was promising to the air that she would quit her hospital nurse job and devote herself to this new work. The I Ching had given her the validation she'd hoped for, and that it happened in Rasa's sanctuary could not be a better augury. He recalled that in the old Chinese, Advancement was called Pushing Upward, and the hexagram was 'ruled' by a steady 'step-by-step process.' Pushing upward are the striplings of every spring, akin to what he'd once called *the proper crocus of April*---the first flower forcing its head up from raw mulch. The phrase was from a poem he'd written twenty years before, and came into his mind apposite.

The time of reverie stalled in the house, with light dying in the bay while outside it seemed expired in the encroaching darkness. These were the sighing moments *between*, but they could neither be grasped nor stayed as they flew along. They were too light to grasp yet too heavy to hold, and in their mercy were unsurpassed. In such twilights, from the asphalt alleys of his childhood, he'd seen nighthawks diving the wrinkles unseen in limpid sky, scouring for bugs with piercing cries. Then, too, was the hour of magic in that world, and in mercy unsurpassed. He'd wanted to hold or stay those moments against the disappointment of day's end, but it was like cupping water in relaxed fingers. More twilights would come, and for them he would always be waiting. And for this one had he not been ready all day? That it came settled on Rasa's cushions was as much an augury for him as her reading had been for Kristan. She had fallen silent, perhaps overcome by the same power, and turned to him for the first time. Her eyes sought his, with a smile revealing a certain feminine insistence, and captured them fair. They held close with each other for minutes, in an accord of understanding. "Just amazing," he whispered with no irony, making her laugh; behind the laugh he saw her eyes acknowledge their feverish night together the year before.

Rasa rose to light the lamps, the celebrate ritual ushering every evening. He watched her moving around, found the joint in the ashtray and stoked it, taking a deep draw. He thought he would go soon, but lingered with Kristan, wanting further communion. Making sure the joint was live, he passed it to her in the near darkness, while holding lightly the hand that would take it. Rasa set a lamp in the middle of the table, and illumination bloomed around them. Shadows dormant in the twilight now swayed sinuously in the corners of the room, and loomed high in the roof. The colors in their skin blushed warmer in the lamplight, and their eyes reflected the sharpened awareness of the magic hour. Though he now drew breath like a nocturnal animal, even with his touching of Kristan and the intuition they shared in close temper, he knew it was Becky he longed for. What was she doing in this replenished night, a few hundred feet away? If the day already seemed long and complete, night was arriving as unstoppable as the waterfall that leapt out of the pool and hung suspended by rainbows in the spray for a moment---but only a trembling moment: there is always time to settle every score.

26

THROUGH THE TWILIGHT OF shadows effaced he made his way,
inching over Rasa's sea wall to the little beach and his back gate,
tossing a glance up the hill to Becky's house. He saw no light
there. Branches of the manzanita lay twisted on the ground, like
the bleached bones of an animal contorted in death. In the scant
minutes of tropical dusk that turn livid before dark, the sky was
spent in the last smolder of fever. Once inside the dimness of his
house, he felt along the counter for the box of wax matches, and
struck one to get his bearings. The lamps from the night before
were in their places, again with blackened globes. When the
match flared out, he dropped it on the floor but stood there in the
born darkness to feel the wrap of solitude. What fortitude there
was in silence; by hearing it, by acquiescing to it, the strength
accumulated might overcome a lot. As life ticked and pulsed
outside---laughter, music, a motor on the bay--- he relished the
clean silence of a moored soul. In the moment, there was no claim
with purchase on him. If Time here was better not fathomed---
who would not forestall it?---sure he heard it, hammering definite
between his arms. He leaned on the counter, and its cool, rich
surface was infinitely soothing to a sweep of his hand. The bay

glimmered softly in crepuscule, and the spell of twilight had subsided to night, another velvet tropical night.

He took the globe off the nearest lamp and lit a match to its wick; in the harsh glare he washed the glass, replaced it with sooty fingers and cranked down the wick. He prepared a few others, and the house quickened with their heartening glows. The best lamp, of heavy, antique-looking fluted glass, he put on the table. It was a fixture in the house for years, of a type no longer sold in the shops. With another match he lit a burner for the pot of beans; they would need another hour of cooking. He sat at the table smoking a Delicado, and leafed through *The Magus*. He recalled where he had left off: Nicholas is at last making love to Julie, it is raining outside, and then the long-awaited rapture dissolves....into betrayal.... He is tied up and drugged by men in black, and.....but.....What a flow of invention, of words! The first night he had been absorbed by this tale, and by the ripe landscape of its Greek island, but now it seemed so entirely beside the point. And what was the point? Well, sheer invention was not the point. Even beautiful phrases were not the point. For truth to be illuminated it must be waylaid, a web of artifice must be spun over a locus frequented by the intended prey. A spinner of tales, like the spider, cannot get by on floating dandelion fluff, however pretty, so must place his web with prescience to snag the prey, the truth. The web is spun from the spider's own substance, and so must words come from substance. Without the prey there is no continuance. It is the human soul that bears truth in discomfort, so needs to be entertained---yes, but also seduced, cajoled, stripped naked in the web and perhaps devoured, to have truth likewise disrobed. Nothing else will do for long. The brilliance of *The Magus* was not such a web; no prey lay palpitating in it, nor did it *expose* truth in its narrative, but rather *played* with it.

So it seemed to him as he thought of his own febrile attempts at writing years before: notebooks filled with phrases, lines of unfinished or failed poems, a paragraph or two here or there; pages and pages, adding up to nothing more than a clogged mind, a blocked imagination, a thwarted heart. Like a fruit that rots before it ripens. At this very table---another nugget!--- he had sat in the last few years stringing ancient beads, fashioning them into jewelry, and turning bamboo into mellifluent flutes---- creative acts--- but never writing. Was a sweet flute as good as a great line of poetry? He permitted himself to answer, out loud: "I hope so." But, as he did not believe it, his soul was no longer untroubled. There was now a claim that had purchase on him, even if it was only by the longing of unfulfilled dreams. The primal origin of his dreams might be found in the wistful rasp of a nighthawk, or in the vault of a black sky with its teams of stars, or just in the praise of his first high school English teacher. No, even as a younger boy he'd treasured the little blank book an uncle had given him. He was in awe of this uncle, who was a foreign correspondent, and of his mother's older sister, for they had lived in Paris before the War. Harold had said, when he handed him the pad, "Now you can write down your thoughts," and it seemed like an injunction. One he did not think he'd obeyed right away, but when he was thirteen he began a journal, and at fifteen was writing maudlin verses. Publishing one in a school newspaper had inspired a trenchant comment from an older schoolmate: the poem was "like cutting up little children." It really only took a moment for him to agree. *It had been.* But he did regret failing to lie that it was just a tweak of the nose he'd intended.

"Which are you drinking---the water or the wave?" Fowles had written (or quoted from Latin) somewhere else, and it was, like all good questions, not as easy to answer as at first it seemed. The wave passed through the water, which did not move with the wave *until it got to shore,* when in the crash they *became one.* Water was life but the wave was mesmerizing. As it was the riddle of substance and form being queried, he knew that to be spellbound was as necessary to his soul as water was to his body. With his mouth he would drink the water but with his eyes he would drink the wave.

Just as complete darkness enveloped the night, Tao sauntered in the front door, and was transfixed by a sphinx moth that buzzed in the 'window' near the jasmine bush. From what other worlds came moth and cat, like emissaries? It was a fancy to imagine their worlds....not like the unplumbed deeps of the sea.... if not fathomless, plainly daunting...... metaphor of the ocean....the watery world....there, below the *waves*, into the *water*....undrinkable sea water!...... But Tao looked from the moth to him, and in her look was something of contempt---or pity---as if she knew the extravagance of his thoughts, and would not countenance them. Then, as if she had decided not much could be done about either him or the moth, she jumped into a chair and settled in with closed eyes----her quiet dismissal was amusing...she, the mother of countless litters. He loved the way she relinquished persistence when it was useless----as often it was! Let the I Ching tell you when perseverance *furthers*. Did she worry about when her kittens would come? He did not think so. The lilies of the field were not the only ones that neither toil nor spin.

He stepped in the garden to peer through the embrace of the *parota* into the heaven of sky. Stars played hide-and-seek, teasing among the branches. Behind the mountain hardly a hint of the moon, which would not appear above the ridge for at least an hour or so; a playful patience would put off his anticipation of it until prompted not to.

27

He pushed aside the book, too impatient to read it any longer: it was wanting in contrast with *this* night as well. Maybe it would suffice as diversion for the return trip. However engrossing the story, and impressive the language, it illuminated nothing essential for him, as did that single curious sentence: *Utram bibis, aqua an undam?* Why was it in Latin? Where had he seen it written? He thought of the music he loved that was 'about' the sea: Debussy's *La Mer*, songs of Elgar, orchestral interludes from Britten's *Peter Grimes*; and he thought of the tales of Joseph Conrad, ones he'd read before setting eyes on any body of water larger than Lake Michigan. But the lake had been an immense presence, like a parent, first in the Dunes in childhood summers; later, when he was confident enough to go off alone, he'd ride his bicycle a couple of miles to sprawl on the huge dressed stone blocks that lined the city lakeshore, and gaze out on the undulant expanse for hours. The lake rotated implacable moods, like Becky: accipient azure one day and scowling verdigris the next, placid or turbulent. Blue ice choked the blocks in cheerful winter sunshine; below vernal cloudbursts it rippled in turquoise laughter. It was there, and under the shady elms of the nearby park, that he turned

impetuous the first astonishing pages of *Walden*. Before turning
the last, he emerged newborn in all but name into an unsuspected
world. Thoreau, floating in his rowboat, tuneful on his flute! He
had cycled over to his friend Reuben's house and shoved the book
into his hands, demanding that he read it: it's way beyond Seton,
he stuttered. And it changed Reuben's life as well.

Fluctuating tides of memory, reliably sweeping in and
dragging out much detritus and driftwood. Unrelenting nostalgia
infiltrated his recollections, insinuating forgotten, or obscure,
experience in them....in his mind he recounted little the life
he was living, but the life he had lived......he did not care that
nostalgia, like melancholy, was not fashionable, very much like
an embarrassment...... Keep your mouth shut and you won't be
embarrassed...... He thought of Menalque, that character in the
fiction of Gide, who announced, "....I do not want to recollect....I
should be afraid of preventing the future and of allowing the past
to encroach on me...." Yes, but only the devil is indifferent to the
past: he *assumes* it harbors the folly and perfidy that furthers him.
And if this was the era of Be Here Now, he *was* here, *now*, waiting,
with the patience of the devil himself, for the appearance of the
moon over the mountain. But it was true, and not unfortunately
so, that the past encroached on him more than did the future,
which is, after all, indefinite, so should be less demanding. *The
breeze blowing from the future* arrives, and on the instant 'dies' to
acquire residence in the past. But that is illusion: "In the Now I
behold the Not-Now," asserted Husserl: there is nothing *but* the
present. *The past is not dead, it's not even past,* said Faulkner. So
if the future is like a consoling illusion, a chimera, the past, far
from preventing it, nearly guarantees it. Have no doubt: it is the
past that lies in wait like an open grave for the future.

If the authenticity of the past was not in question, how could
it be otherwise? The thick, salt and pepper hair on his head was
once thin brown fuzz, and he did not speak English when he was
born; nor could he then whittle with simple tools a bamboo flute.
Once he had gotten a mysterious fortune cookie in a Chinese

restaurant. It read: "Someone from your past will reenter your past." What strange gnosis had that come from? Or was it just like a Borgesian paradox? How many torturing paradoxes turned out to be more telling than simple facts? So what if mathematics was the language of scientific speculation? Only the cells spoke that language---- the molecules, the atoms. The cosmos might have been invented in that language, but we, contingent beings, spoke the language of nostalgia, the proper language of the dying that is life. But Menalque had gone on to say, "It is out of the utter forgetfulness of yesterday that I create every new hour's freshness." Lucky him, to forget yesterday---if you believe him! And perhaps the sun won't rise tomorrow if you forget yesterday! But it was not lucky; it was the wish of a fettered soul, sillier than jousting at windmills. Nothing fresh can arise but out of the past, sure not the infant thrust from the womb. The flute that comes with skill from the stick of bamboo takes form from the past. *Now* is a garden of the past.... trite metaphor!.....and here's another, a simile... The breeze blowing from the future caresses that garden, like a mother's hand smoothing the blanket on her sleeping child.... Daedelus tells Theseus in another fable of Gide's that Ariadne's thread in the labyrinth "will be your link with the past....from which what you are to be must spring."---- as if only heroes and gods deserved the future.

He lit another cigarette, another Delicado. The oval shaped smoke with the spinsterish bust of a woman printed on the wrapper, unchanged for decades. Definitely not in the modern style. While they were in every tienda, he hardly knew anyone else who smoked them. The antique look of the package, and only eighteen inside. The cheap price that might well turn out to be expensive. He did not want to know what he knew.

The sky had brightened, and the wind whispered in the eaves. A mere gust of wind, especially a mere gust of wind, moved him, thrilled him, as if it might be a signal message from some spirit or demiurge. *Many a wind is like a son to me*, sang Rilke. And omens were to be read everywhere. Once, a few years before, he had been sitting at the table on another night of high moonlight, when he saw stealing into the garden a thin human form. He went out and encountered Julian, the villager from a small hut just above his, and he was aiming a rifle up into the *parota*. "What are you doing?" he demanded. Julian was a wiry, intense fellow with a wife and small son too, and he muttered in a warning, breathless voice that a *bruja* was hiding in the tree and had to be shot because it was a bad omen. He did not know what to say, but tried to mollify him as he stalked the witch. Soon a shot popped off, and from a lofty branch a large bird fluttered to the ground. It was an owl, twitching its last in the gloaming. Julian chortled in satisfaction and, grabbing the dead bird, went back up to his hut. There he saw, hushed in the shadows of their doorway, his woman holding the infant in her arms. He stood in the garden a few minutes longer, realizing that he had never seen an animal shot dead in front of him. Still shaking, he returned to the table, to his wife and infant boy waiting there.

And had it been coincidence or a parallel, but joyful, omen that only half an hour before his son had spoken his first word? He'd carried him in his arms to the garden where Nico had pointed a chubby finger to the sky, pursed his lips and clearly pronounced----not *dada* or *mama*, but *moon*.

28

OVER THE ROOF OF Rasa's house the distant lights of the hotel were flickering fitfully; its generator could be temperamental. The waves rolled in with agreeable *whooshes*, a sound as if the rocks were only pebbles, and snatches of talking and laughing drifted loose in the night.

How fitting that Rasa was home; he'd missed her. He could not tell if Kristan was still there. Moonlight washed the hillside above the hotel, so it couldn't be long before the moon itself sailed into the clockwork sky. He thought of cautious Galileo who, after renouncing at the Inquisition his belief that the Earth moved, muttered under his breath that it *did* move--- the last word of science was not worth a life. But the seeming motion of the stars and planets around the Pole Star had the appearance of a perfect clock, so the illusion of a central, stationary Earth was compelling, an error solaced by a peculiar equity. Far more comprehensive than poetic license, symbolic language vivified, or justified, yearnings of the soul that could not be forestalled by sober rationality. *He did not want to know what he knew.* This was not a mechanism of defiance, much less of denial; rather, it was the taste of fancy that, in a pleasure of exuberance, liberated poetry and song from stubborn reason and gave them the freedom of dance. What used to be called the Music of the Spheres was nothing if not dance; the atoms and the stars danced, as the human body danced, to the same music. Deaf Beethoven heard it. Only death does not hear it, though it wants to. And while you might not dance *about* architecture, you would *for* it. Shiva danced the world into being, and in the Torah, the Word that was in the beginning was not *words* but a thrumming of vibration that excited the atoms to whirl as if in delirium, like dervishes.

As he was plunged into these thoughts, a slim spotlight penetrated the leafy limbs of the *parota*; a wedge of moon jabbed over the mountain ridge, and garden shadows began their dance in the breeze, as if the moon alone had given them life. Yet the moon gave only a pensive reflection of the great incandescence on the other side of the world, but the speechless, chalky light soaked into him so deeply it seemed he could taste it, a bittersweet juice. Clockwork had brought it over the mountain to hang in his tree like an oval lantern, and the wind-sprung branches made it seem to swivel. He sat riveted by the shadows a while; then the swooning wind ceased, and the world was breathless; the small waves bounced in the bay now with nowhere to go....

....He lowered the wick on the lamp to have the moonlight brighter. The moth, gone for a while, was back; perhaps it had drunk, or rested. Tao turned her head to look, but was unmoved. She twitched when a dog barked nearby, and there was a burst of confused sounds of people shouting somewhere. Music blared out suddenly, but subsided at once to a low rumble. The multitudes of night could not hide, even with burning lamps, from the mothering moon. Somewhere in the night, he knew, promises were spoken that would not be kept. But he knew there was nothing that could degrade the perfection, nor break the promise, of this white evening he'd traveled far to have.

29

Without warning, Becky flew up the steps into the doorway, swiveling on tiptoe as if in alarm, hair flying, puffing a cigarette. Her figure was silhouetted against the sparkling bay, face too shadowed to read. But he could read her body, which, unlike a *prepared* face, dissembles not easily. In the sway of it was confusion, yearning, questioning. He rose and went to her with arms out, but she flinched before yielding to them. He pulled her to the table and in the lamplight her face was a troublous mask, far different than the one he had seen in bed. Her expression seemed to struggle with cureless words before these rushed out, in a dismissive grunt, "I've torn up so many drawings today…I can't work…my head is breaking. I know you leave soon and I don't have the time for this….but I want it…anyway…" She left off, raised her arms high with hands flapping, as if submitting to a pat down, then jumped up to the kitchen, looking wildly all around. She swirled back to swagger in front of him, arching her back like the dare of a matador. If her manner were not so distressed he would have thought it comical.

"Do you want a glass of water----or how about some raicilla?" He could not tell if he was more annoyed or pleased by her appearance, her attitude. "Water," she cried, and he went to pour out a glass from the pottery jug where he kept it. He carried it to her, now slouched in the chair opposite Tao, who had opened her eyes to watch them, unruffled. She drained it quickly and straightened up to say, "This is….how do you say in English?…a lark. It doesn't mean anything to you…maybe it doesn't mean anything….to me….all I want is to work, but I liked your body in the night, and you will go. You will go and come back with someone else…" With her head down, more words trailed off, too garbled to hear. Was it resignation, anger, longing or fear? Had he misread the situation?--- not such a surprise really. She had slung one leg over the other knee, and it was jouncing like a metronome, as if to keep time with her turmoil.

"Wait, Becky, listen, what's a lark? Think of the songster itself…. *alouette* in French, right?…Sure, there is a slang, and it means having a merry old time, just for the fun of it. So what! The lark is a beautiful, free creature that pours out its life in song---- 'unpremeditated art' in Shelley's poem--- and we could do worse, couldn't we?" *Unpremeditated.* That's it! But he knew he was pleading his case to keep *their* lark free of psychology, so that it did not violate the matching lark of the week itself. Really? As if the week could be free of psychology and simply a pure exercise in *Zen!* Here was an illusion he was determined to defend--- but was he using her to defend it? Still, for him there was no particular anguish even in *that*---which was fine, because he had plenty elsewhere. And this time, this time at least, his own *because* was so much better than her *because.*

"Yes, yes, you're right, eat and drink and be….be….."she laughed, but he saw she was still in agitation, and he hardly knew what else might be done to pacify it. Instead, he went to the kitchen and brought back the bottle of *raicilla*, with limones and glasses. "Let's have a drink," he said, with as neutral a tone as he could manage, filling the glasses. He coaxed onto her face the same kind of smile he had on his----a better mask?----and prompted her to drink down the liquor with him. Neither smelling nor tasting good, it went down with a jolt close to hallucination, and quickly circulated a probing heat through his body. For a minute his thoughts fused in a melt that left him giddy, and in a voice brightly flippant he declaimed a couplet from Blake:

> He who binds to himself a joy
> Does the winged life destroy.

He was delighted with himself for remembering this correspondence, and let go a giggle in the moon-washed house, noting how he sounded too much like Melman. Becky seemed to have lost her agitation, and was quiet, even somnolent, in the chair, but then he thought she was gathering herself for something. For tears or for laughter?

"What did you do today? Did you go down to the beach?" The two questions floated out into the room where he still heard the echo of Blake's lines---though she'd ignored them---but leveled his voice to tell her of his time above the waterfall and his visit to Rasa. While he talked he poured more raicilla in their glasses, but she waved it away heedless, so he threw down the next shot by himself, reinforcing the warmth in his blood and the flurry in his head.

"I've never been up there, it is good, yes?" She had definitely brightened, and with these words, beginning to sound compliant, he heard again the inflections of rural Belgium, and tried to picture the kind of life she had there as a girl in Art school. But it was no go, he could not see past the woman in the lamplight, whose usual animation had returned. The raicilla was working in her too, and he understood that the alleviation of her dejection--- if it was that, rather than a nutshell jealousy---was sorely needed for *this* lark to be in fact the *same* lark he had portrayed. Years ago, when his friend Ken was having marital troubles, he had said to him, "If you can't have a ball, forget it." Ken accused him of heartlessness, which perhaps it was, but in fact their marriage had crumbled anyway. Later, his own had fallen apart too, leaving a divided child. A casualty of his indifference? Or was it his refusal to allow the soar of the lark to be interrupted by the fallibility of troubled psyches? And what of the other? Had she no part, no complicity? There was no shortage of fault anywhere, so it was too convoluted to untangle. *More power in relish than in doubt*----so had he thought yesterday. And, as it was still the best motto for the heart compromised by the vacillation of feelings, he repeated it to Becky, who had gotten up and was weaving again in the doorway. She just walked over to him this time and asked, "What is this 'relish'?" "It's like enjoyment, zest, pleasure in taste," he answered, adding that he would say the lark *relished* its flight in song, or she her work on paper. And that he relished being here, and being with her. "Yes, I like this word, I see what you mean. Why not?" With a flourish of gayety, she picked up the glass of *raicilla* from the table, gulped it with a gasp, and trailed out into the garden while singing lines he thought were Flemish. She danced in pirouettes, joining the company of shadows; moonlight brushed her hair to silken white.

Seeing her there, his heart soared now like the lark of poetry, and he went into the garden to join her and dance together. Under the regalement of the moon flooding through the reach of the parota they grew gay with intoxication. It seemed he had more than recaptured the mood of last night, had bettered it, and was filling again with appetite, with desire, wanting the taste of living flesh. He pulled her close for a kiss and just stood there with her, rocking in place. He did not see her face---what mask it might be wearing---but he knew her body was humming in the music of desire too; he could not believe how what he felt, or *thought*, had been transferred with such startling ease to her, and that she had received it so----what?----willingly. Now the marvel of the night repeated in them, and gladly this was no illusion.

Without a word, he took her by the hand and led her out the gate and down to the gully to stand her before the datura. "You brought me a flower last night," she murmured. "It was almost open this morning." The white bells were ominous in the moonlight, a fatal beauty against the dark green leaves. A dainty trickle purled in the creek, passing the silent and dark cottage; whatever spirits were as if drugged. There were lights and voices in Rasa's house, and thick shadows in the lot before it. Someone stepped out from the kitchen and seemed to call to them, but they stood very still and did not answer. Soon, it was she who drew him back to the house and, frowning at his spindly bamboo bed, begged him to come to hers, with its good mattress and mosquito net. He agreed, and said he'd bring some food too. "No more *raicilla*," she said, "I still have some *mota*."

But when she left, he had one more shot of it, then gathered up some things in the net bag, and took the beans off the stove to set on the wall by the door, so he wouldn't forget. The moon was bright in the branches, gibbous as en egg; it was getting late, the shadows outside shortened. A few restless birds trilled in the little manzanita shrub out front, and he sat for a few minutes at the table, to collect himself and breathe alone. He did not know which surprised him more----his credulity or his incredulity. He had turned her from morose woman to sprightly girl in a matter of minutes with few words. Why was that surprising? In sincerity true as breath, he believed every word he had said. This was his truth, and if she was his prey he was hers. The pressing tangle of their bodies in passion was no less truth than was their dance in the garden; nor was it more. Appetite was less arguable than love, unless it was the love of the saints. And in the final analysis---if there could ever be one---appetite *was* love, cause for the cry of the life force to continue. Appetite, repulsion, attraction, adhesion.....universal entropies to which everything was subject, from which nothing was exempt. He could not have foreseen what was happening; neither would he prevent it. So he left the house with a light step and paused again on the outcropping at Becky's gate; Punta Mita floated far away on the pencilled horizon, luminous as a paper cutout stuck there, and the pelicans asleep on their Rock under enshrining light had the appearance of minikin icons.

30

A SWOOP OF RAUCOUS MOON parrots---dropping to the foliage only long enough to inflict their shrill vexations on the nearby--- woke him. In racket they came, in racket they went. Or perhaps it was the ring of a quarrel that flew from the village. Or the ranchero playing on the cantina jukebox---which might have been playing all night. One-eyed Luis would do that when he was on a bender. It was a jaunty tune about a *caballero* who carved his *novia's* name in a maguey cactus, so to have her celebrated later in a bottle of tequila! It rolled through the air and bothered no one, or no more than did the roar and hum of Manhattan in the middle of the night. Rising and falling on the breeze, mostly swallowed in the open world of the bay. Though he avoided noise, it was away enough to have, perversely, a kind of charm.

From a dead sleep he found a morning full-blown. Through the mosquito net he saw Becky at her easel, vaguely mumbling as she slashed her crayons across the paper. He watched her quietly, and remembered the roisterous clinches of *their* long night, cosmic as any embrace of demiurges. She danced even as she worked, waltzing away from the easel and squinting at the image; like a rash artist in a movie, her motions were sometimes graceful, sometimes clumsy. He drew open the net and lumbered out groggy, trying not to look too obviously at the easel. But she exclaimed, "Ooh, you're up at last. Look!" He came up to her and saw that it was a drawing of a man lying in bed seen through a mosquito net. He did not recognize himself in the figure, but knew it was a generic study that succeeded in conveying the impression of a profound sleep unto death. It was evocative, seen even in his dopiness, and he wondered if he should have it. "I waited for you... for breakfast....but I now made coffee," she warbled, and brought him a cup.

He pondered the drawing as he sipped the coffee, while Becky busied herself in the kitchen---getting breakfast he hoped. There were few colors, and the lines were deft and spare in a modernist style. "You like it?" she shouted from the kitchen. "Don't tear up this one," he answered. She laughed, and danced plates of food to the table. "Don't worry, be hungry," she said, improving the yogi's advice.

He put on the pants thrown to the floor, shaking them out for scorpions, and sat at the worktable she'd swept clear. The bay was bright through the open side of the house, at whose brink she had teetered the other night. The Lucinda was not to be seen, so he knew it was later than usual; *ni modo*, the villagers would say. They ate, but Becky jumped up and down, puttering here and there, in what seemed to him disorder. He took a second cup of coffee outside to the little patio, where he'd feel the sky over his head, and be dazed by the hillside thrashing of coco palms in the wind; far up there, the little parrots squawked. The day was still fresh, as if just out of a box and popped from the cellophane wrap. He reflected again how this newness got repeated from a small repertory, and was hardly vitiated by its familiarity. Nature, which seems so mindless to those whose internal chatter is glutted by ennui, to him seemed reverberant from the machinations of a grinning god; a god whose impanation had steamed on the breakfast plates, who snickered at Man's love of theories fascinating but futile. The set of the world here had every element of human invention; nothing willful or arbitrary lasted long, yet everything had steadiness of will. In saying less, it meant more. If the world he saw and heard now was less pristine than the one yesterday above the waterfall, it was not any the less affecting. Though its full measure could not be taken, it did not seem so; he would gather it all: the sky, the water, the palms, the house, the woman----and himself. If he was indulging in self -congratulation for such wisdom he forgave himself by not displaying it to anyone.

Becky was still at the easel, happily working, oblivious of everything else; her plate was hardly touched. He dropped his dishes in the sink, gathered his things together, and stood around for a few minutes to test her absorption: it was solid, almost unnerving. With a hug he gave goodbye. She kissed him, but went on with her drawing.

The lamps in his house were low and blackened, and he blew them out, this time putting them all on the counter by the sink. He took a bracing shower, shaved, made some more coffee, swept the floor, watched the pangas in the bay. It was the third morning, and he was ready to repeat unspoiled the day before. With the narcotic of youth not yet depleted, he wanted to let himself go in a flattering innocence not bothered by moralizing. In its grace and bounty the world shall provide the same day for choosing. The habit of belief, the habit of doubt. The sun rose, will set later, will rise tomorrow. In a different time, he'd get involved in repairs or projects. But these were to be days *hors de commerce:* he would be as idle as he liked, insouciant, and not waste time doing anything---possibly not even think of the hourglass.

31

A FAUCET IS SLOWLY DRIPPING, thudding in a large, gleaming white porcelain sink. The only other sound in the room is the debile huff of his breathing, a wheeze in the empty space. He is standing nearby, listening to the rhythm, which in his mind he characterizes as "normal". He repeats the word, this time out loud, feeling comforted, but immediately the sound is amplified while its rate increases with irritating urgency. He bends over the sink and grips the faucet's key to shut it off, but it will not budge. The key has a curious, rough, rocklike feel---- "stubborn" is the word he pronounces--- and as he continues to apply himself to shutting off the dripping water, coarse sand replaces the drops and the thudding turns into the ticking of a clock, the kind of clock that, from the dispiriting walls of his public school room, seemed to stall the hours. Astonished and dismayed, he lurches up from the sink, and weighs the belief that he is working on a solution against the sense of impasse when he hears a strident voice say, "We can do nothing about that faucet, don't you know? It's better to give it up. Go look out the window." The voice is familiar, he knows who it is, but can't remember the name. Nor does he see a window anywhere in the room. Just for something to do, he puts a cupped hand under the faucet to collect some sand, but it all flows right through to the sink anyway, and then to the drain, even as water would. But the feel of the sand running off his palm is sensuous, hypnotic, and he is fading, falling asleep.......

.... The insinuation of dawn, confused impressions persisting in his head. So it was another day. Was it the next day or the next...or the next? Coming from his dreams---a faucet dripping sand?---he did not know. The sky in the west was still luminous from the waning moon sunk behind the mountain. Time not worth measuring had begun in its own way to fracture, and he had lost track of the sand in the hourglass. *Sand.* He had not seen Becky for a day---or was it longer?--- and did not care to make out the reason. Oh, he had gone again above the waterfall, and to the beach yesterday to have a breakfast of fish at the hotel. He remembers a silly conversation with Rick the Stick. Rick was a retired American Army sergeant raising his two children from a failed marriage, and the swagger stick he carried, together with the trim goatee he sported, insisted on his military stance. He did not reveal much about himself, but never failed to make sardonic comments about local matters. To Rick, Mexico would never amount to anything "as long as its *banos* don't work." He sat eating his fish and listened to a sour diatribe, while wishing he would see Octavio. There were one or two small projects that needed to be accomplished while he was gone, work he had thought of in spite of his resolve to do nothing. He hoped Octavio would somehow turn up at the right moment.

The bed yawed from his turning over, and a few birds had begun their chattering early; it seemed they'd awakened to keep him company. Time had certainly not disappeared, because there was an airline ticket in his bag on the *banco*. Was it for tomorrow or the next day? When he got up to make coffee, he would look. But he was not sure what day *this* was, so he'd have to ask in the village, or ask Rasa.

The chill in the air induced pleasing sensations, delectable but tinged with melancholy---the hazard of nostalgia, not of yearning. How was it that in the coursing of time--- days fleet but not seeming so---a steady river into which we sometimes step not even once, but stagger more asleep than awake, marks are put upon us, marks that get hidden but not erased? After thousands of days these marks reemerge intact, like the grimace on a drowned victim sunk by weights. If all our days are numbered----so many running days---who knows the number? He would rather know that someone does than know the number himself. Had the impetus for this thought come from some dream before the faucet of sand? Why should we need the 'symbols' of dreams decoded? No, such fleeting realities wanted the drowse of bedclothes to stay alive, and dissolved in the air, leaving just a structure in the subconscious able to support new dreaming. *I'm forever blowing bubbles.* Could the history of a soul be told by its dreams alone? Maybe it was only the soul itself that could know, or care.

For a long while he listened to the rhythmic clamor of waves dashing on the rocks and beach below, giving it close attention. It was not paced in the monotony of a metronome, but had its own inflections, like speech. There were pauses, hesitations…then eagerness, a hurrying, an emphasis. Sometimes softer, sometimes louder. One of the movements of Debussy's *La Mer* was titled "The Dialogue of the Wind and the Wave". *Dialogue.* What he heard at the waterfall, what he heard in the wind, what he heard now, was speech. Animals talked; stone struggled to consciousness through wavelengths longer than millennia. That speech was in a frequency far too slow for the human ear, too slow for any ear. But the planet heard it; the planet heard everything. Man is, or has, the nerve endings of the planet, taunted barely sentient by high-frequency data from distant Space to be transformed for the planet's use. *Transcend, transmute, transfigure,* and especially, *transform*---wonderful words wading in a swamp of uncertain extent where enigmatic signposts point in ambiguous directions. The dictionary will tell you what each word signifies, a useful hint for converse, but what do they actually mean? The dictionary is not a philosopher.

He jumped out of bed and turned up the lamp he'd left burning low on the table. He slipped on his *huaraches* against the cold floor, tamping them first. He put on the coffee, slipped into the garden to peer at the sky, where stars were flickering out in diffused light, and the new morning. A meteor shot brilliant behind the branches of the parota and sputtered into the hills. Did he only imagine a tiny explosion? It seemed like a revelation and gladness choked up in his throat, banishing the last trace of melancholy. He pushed away the mystery of dreams, unresolved as they would always be. If they contained instructions they were meant for sleep, the darkest work yet to be done. He sensed the night wind coming downriver shift, and the world, so meshed in colliding mysteries, enlarged for its morning. There were many fresh birds greeting it, and out on the big Rock he made out a pelican fluffing its wings in a marvelous stretch.

The coffee tasted unusually good, smoking his first Delicado, gluttonous for the light coming up fast. It was a delicious, selfish but watchful obsession. There was no one around to whom he'd owe excuses. Not even Tao was around. Normal sounds were coming from the village, the bay, the trees, and he relished being used to them.

32

HEADING OUT TO THE Point he stopped indecisive on the stone platform at the bottom of Becky's steps. He did not want to ignore her, but he also did not want to give her the chance to come out with him. Reluctantly, he pulled the cord but did not hear the bell ring in the house. He tried again, weakly. There was no answer. If she'd gone out she hadn't roused him either, so he continued down the path, which narrowed for a hundred yards to hug the hillside, winding out by another creek that came down steeply into a grotto darkened over by another ancient parota. An elegantly designed and trimmed palapa sat on one side above the creek, just behind the gnarled old leafy tree. With only intermittent light filtering through the ravine, the scene might have looked creepy if not for a hollowed niche in the tree trunk where a black pottery statue of the *Virgen de la Soledad* serenely nestled. A votive candle sat before it, balefully smoking as if just blown out. Don Pepe Diaz lived in the house, grandson of Mexico's long dead dictator; like the infamous old man, Pepe had a love for all things French. As a boy, Pepe had grown up in his grandfather's Parisian exile. His air of condescension was tolerated with amusement by the villagers, who called him *ladeado* because he always held his head tilted to one side. Looming dramatically high above Pepe's house was another, of Isadora, who rented rooms to transients and backpackers; from there had come the file of busted pot smokers that time. The house had been abandoned before she took it over, and in his first year he used to climb up to it and sit dreamily looking out on the bay. While he simmered beans in a clay *olla* over a grate fired with twigs and coco husks, he'd play one of his small cane flutes brought from Trinidad.

Only a couple of years ago, Isadora had sent someone to him with a request to come and look at something for her. She'd taken him outside to an embankment where half a dozen ceramic figurines sat in the dirt at the feet of two dark men with inscrutable expressions. Isadora did not know what to make of these objects, which the older of the two men said, in spare words, were ancient. As far as he knew, no ancient objects had ever been found in the vicinity, but the old man said they came from higher up in the mountains, from a *tumba*. He picked one up, five or six inches in size, a reddish-brown female figure with grotesque features, inspected it thoughtfully, trying not to give away his own ignorance. The price seemed cheap, cheaper than fragments he had bought in foolish afternoon shadows at Monte Alban. Though he hardly had a clue, an impulse prompted him to overcome, or just ignore, his doubts. Was it 'the courage of trust' or blind faith----or plain gullibility? No, it was none of these. It was the desire, goaded by that imp of the perverse that could never be wholly suppressed, to reach farther than he thought he could grasp. He felt giddy to take a chance, which was easy, rather than not take a chance, which was easier. And do it knowing that, in Mallarme's words, *one throw of the dice will never abolish chance.* So with a certain thrill----others might say greed trying to avenge fear----he found himself bargaining with the campesino and telling Isadora he thought the pieces were good, they should buy them all. She bought two and he the rest. By the time he knew *they* were all clever replicas, he'd gone on to buy real ones elsewhere, and his new career had vindicated that

'throw of the dice'---a throw that would acquire the legend and
mark of a milestone.

He continued on the path through the grotto until it abruptly
disappeared into the rocks of the bay itself. There was nothing
to do but leap from rock to rock, or boulder, often having to
wait for the swells to slough off. He passed the round palapa
built virtually on the rocks atop a huge retaining wall, also in
the crotch of a steep canyon, where Cindy lived. In storms,
rocks fell into the roof, which was kept in frequent repair. And
what of the anxiety of the dwellers? Finally, the trail followed a
narrow passage over a rise and emerged around the Point into a
small meadow where, before the trail thinned to nothing, stood
the house of Corinne. Beyond was the virgin jungle, until a few
miles farther another smaller beach cove appeared; it was only ten
minutes by panga, and behind the beach were clustered the simple
huts of Pisota, a fishing village pure and simple with no outsiders.
The fishermen spoke a rustic Spanish and were friendly if shy, and
used sometimes to land on his little beach to sell him a bucket
of oysters, fat enough for knife and fork. He had gone there the
year before, with his friend Kate and several day-trippers, bringing
plenty of food and drink and pot for the day. A panga let them
off in the morning and came back for them in late afternoon. The
sand on the beach was fine, mounded Sahara-like in drifts, and it
was only their long-bronzed bodies that kept off sunburn. The day
was like a South Seas idyll, but some of the fishermen's children
came out to watch them with wonder, so they had to comport
themselves with more discretion than was their wont.

Corinne's house was set in the meadow up from the bay, in
a level, lush garden she had installed. Thatched with costly royal
palm trucked down from Nayarit, it had the effect he imagined
of an English country cottage. He whistled as he walked through
the careful landscaping up to the patio, and thought she was
not at home. She had bought or financed Seferino's panga, and
could embark to the beach or the resort town from her own rocky
landing when the bay was not too rough. But she appeared in

the doorway just as he got near, greeting him without surprise, as if he had not been unexpected. She was wearing a long hand woven Indian huipil and the same rope sandals as Martita, but she was not flouncing or twirling demurely. She was taking care of business, and, as he entered the house, she asked him if he knew the paintings of Hundertwasser, and picked up a small book from the single table in the room and handed it to him. He hadn't, but leafed through the book with some interest. The artist reminded him vaguely of Klimt and while he made some aimless comments Corinne resumed whatever puttering she had been doing before his interruption. Taking care of business seemed to be Corinne's forte. She was an intelligent, carefully groomed woman who knew exactly what she was doing even if you didn't. He sat down at the table, continued to look through the book, and felt only slightly awkward. He did not want to be put off by the lack of ceremony, no hint of badinage or curiosity, so he forced himself to speak with an exaggerated offhandedness.

"I was hoping you'd be here. Otherwise, I might have gone down to sit in the studio house." This was a guest house by the boat landing, set right at the water's edge, completely open, with a low wall of sea rocks hopefully keeping out the waves.

"I heard you were here. I saw Becky yesterday."

"She's been doing some good work," he managed to say.

"I was going to make tea. Would you like some?"

"Sure. I would. Thanks." Even to him, this offhandedness was tiresome; if she'd seen Becky, probably she *knew*; he didn't mind. Though Corinne was a woman who took care of business but never tipped her hand, he was still hopeful that something might break out in good time. She was pretty, honey blonde, a blueblood from a swank suburb, and was now smoothly preparing tea and a plate of cookies at the counter while talking of the house she was going to build on the hill behind for her parents. "They love to spend a few weeks here from time to time. I can use it for guests or rent it out," she said. Everything delivered matter of fact.

"What day is today? I've lost track of time."

"It's Friday. The 16th." She brought over the tea and cookies.

"Who's doing the work for the house?"

"Camarino is overseeing it. It's his land. He's got brothers and nephews to do the work. It's a big job. Much bigger than my house. And of course, they'll want it pretty closed in. Sort of an outpost Winnetka!" She poured the tea, giving a discreet laugh, perhaps so he wouldn't think she necessarily approved of their measures. "Why did you want to know the day?"

"Because it tells me I have to go back tomorrow. I looked at my ticket this morning. Short trip this time, kind of unexpected. I love full moon here, so I took the chance I got to come for it."

"It is beautiful. You know, I'm going in tomorrow myself. We could pick you up on your beach, but it will be early."

"Great, that works, I'm up early."

"About 8. We're going all the way to the Rosita. Just give Sef some pesos for the gas. I need things for the house, but I want to get back for lunch; I have workers. Tom was here, did you see him?"

"No. Too bad. How is he?" Tom was her old boyfriend from back home, who hung out now and then without cramping her style.

"Not very good. He just had a close call in Mazatlan. Conner didn't come through. He was supposed to have the mule loads by the airstrip at a certain time, but wasn't there. They waited for him, but then the wrong police showed up, so they had to take off in a hurry and almost crashed it. But the police waited, clever bastards. When Conner finally came down the mountain with the load, his campesinos spotted them in time, and they all split into the hills. The cops got the whole load." And as she told the story, his mind went over the numerous schemes he had been privy to with Tom and Conner, never gutsy enough to get himself included, but also held back by his own fear or timidity. Her account was more detailed than he would care to remember. Now he was not sure which he regretted less----his lack of guts or his fear. Was there much difference? As she talked, scenes passed in his mind of figures creeping or lurking about in the shadows, while a mysterious power launch bobbed at anchor near Conner's catamaran during another full moon. They were Tom's cronies from Aspen or Newport Beach. One of them gave him some white powder that turned out to be a powerful tranquilizer; inhaling only a little of it turned him into a zombie. He had given it away to Barry, who shared some with Corinne when they were together for a time. A full circle of sorts! He felt a decided uneasiness thinking of all this, of his skirting for years the company of marijuana outlaws, without ever being one. A small packet of *kif* smuggled in his underwear on the Tangier-Gibraltar ferry was the biggest chance he'd ever taken, years before.

Brightening up, he teased Corinne: "Remember the piperadine?"

"Piperadine? Was that the stuff we snorted? Barry and I called it pepperoni, and it was terrible, terrible! We didn't know what hit us." She laughed with a *heh heh* sound that almost made him laugh, but he pressed on.

"I didn't know what it was when Peterson gave it to me. I snorted some at night when Donna and the baby were sleeping, and it put me into an idiot state where nothing mattered. Reality seemed pointless, and the 'perfume' of the drug incapacitated my will, like the perfume Gide has wafting in the labyrinth of the Minotaur. If a monster can be pacified, imagine the effect on a mortal."

"I know. We were scared at first, but then Barry got into one of his joke routines, so we had a pretty good time---- but we never took it again."

"Well, I got to the point where it seemed very Zen to me. A chemical Zen, but then acid is a chemical satori."

"That's an illusion. Like your illusion that Santos is a Buddhist." He was stung, stunned by this, but found a voice to plead anyway: "I've watched Santos, he's in the zone. He moves deliberately, and his mind knows what's next, so his body wastes no energy."

"Maybe, but he also beats his children, and works Carmela to death. He's mean to Rasa."

"He's Mexican, with the Spanish Catholic weight on him trampling the Indian soul. All I say is there is a Buddhist disposition----or maybe I mean Taoist. In different circumstances he'd be making the 'Journey to the East'."

"Bullshit," she growled, and got up to end the line of conversation.

"I've never heard Rasa complain," but he knew how weak that retort was even when saying it; Rasa *complained* of little. He felt cowed by the rebuff, but still had to wonder if his louche romanticism about Santos was justified. Corinne did not have to raise ten children---born every year, some died, he had no count----on hand caught fish, hand harvested coconuts, a little rent money from Rasa. He remembered the early years, when he watched him go out at dawn in his canoe and come back hours later with fish flopping in the bottom. Seldom enough to sell after presumably feeding the kids. But always with quiet demeanor, the quiet dignity, as he saw it, of living off the land. *The salt of the earth.* Corn and beans and fish. Excess fish bartered for bananas or tomatoes or whatever, if he was lucky. Buddhist? Taoist? His own naive projection?

He got up too, and wandered out into Corinne's back garden, blinking in the fierce sunlight, munching on the last cookie, and breathed deeply to void the mood. Corinne was talking about Hundertwasser again, and he pretended to pay attention, but he was anxious to go. "Anyone staying in the Studio house?" he asked. When she said no, he just wandered down to take a look. It was a quite small, round palapa, with a bed on a ledge, a tiny bathroom and a two- burner stove. A small table and two chairs. He sat there for a while, and imagined rough weather inundating it. Only the hotel side of the beach was visible, but it was distant, indistinct. He could hear no village sounds, and the sense of isolation combined with tidy comfort was thorough. At this level the waves that crashed on the rocks were loud and alarming, and they were the only sounds he heard. The sound of his thoughts were tamped far down, their muddle thankfully muted, yet harboring the disquiet impression there was something he'd never learned.

He went back up to the house, where Corinne was now working absorbed at the table, taking care of business. "Thanks for the tea," he said, patting her shoulder lightly. "Nice of you to come by," she replied, pausing only slightly at her work. "See you in the morning---better be ready! We can't wait."

He rushed along the path, stopping to look at the Virgin in the tree trunk niche. The votive candle was burning low without smoke: someone had relit it. The gurgle of the cool, dark creek was nice after the heat of the trail. A cat sprinted in the brush, chasing a lizard. When he got to the rocks that were the path for a bit, waves were pounding in and he did not avoid getting wet. He mounted the boulder in front of Becky's gate and without a second thought yanked the bell pull. He heard it ring this time, and Becky soon pranced out to the kitchen patio, spirited and laughing. "I'm in a good time, drawing!" she shouted. "How about dinner at the Yacht Club?" he hollered back, "I'm leaving tomorrow." "Yes, yes! I'll come by before dark. I think I want some of that raicilla." And she disappeared into the house. Suddenly everything appeared easy. Tao was sitting on the front doorstep as he got through the gate, cleaning herself. She paused to stare in his direction.

33

Whatever satisfaction he got from his long indulged propensity for doubt, he took little pleasure in it, whereas the propensity for faith had pleasure, but little satisfaction. If what together they culled was a paradox, that gave something to hold, even in standstill, while waiting to confront the conundrum of identity. Ambivalence could only end in a curse, an abdication by frowning---the headaches of the wrinkled brow. And though doubt might be durable, it had slight power, while faith---its power sometimes great---always had selvedges of deception. *I don't want belief, I want knowledge,* the knight confessed to Death---disguised as a cowled monk---in *The Seventh Seal.* Was that the secret?--- both doubt and faith carried far as the brink of knowing delight and abandoned there: neither is needed for singing, dancing, loving-----praising, relishing all-----and these had power. He saw that Becky gained power through her struggles, but did Corinne have power? He thought not. She was a woman who took charge, but it was not power she had, but dominion. The power he wanted was particularly not from 'control', but more from 'out–of-control'. The protection of control denied access to the divine; defenseless, letting go gave it. Whether ineffable or not, he knew that all these words fell into a swale of ambiguities themselves, but if he knew what he meant, or what he decided he meant, he would not fall in after them. His disagreement with Corinne--- personality clash?---was over meaning. *Meaning!* Power had a feel, a taste and fragrance, that freed him from words---and freed him *for* them. *I do not sing because I am happy, I am happy because I sing.* An unmistakable meaning.

Here he was lying in the hammock, and Tao had actually jumped into his lap, unborn litter and all. He banished from his mind the farrago of words---spilled out during the burdensome practice of judging---and studied the roof plaits, while from the shimmer of afternoon sunlight he imagined harpsichord music tinkling out. Landowska was bent over the keys in a black dress, hair in a French bun, playing with a seraphic smile Rameau or Couperin. The music was infinitely delicate, showering through the myriad leaves of the parota. He saw her face turn raptly from the keys to glance at him, lifting a limp hand at the end of a phrase with a flourish, an eidolon of antique grace. She charmed him, and he was surprised, even shocked, at how vivid the image was. The music sifted through agitated fragments of sunlight, but seemed detached from *her* harpsichord. He felt the weight of the cat on his stomach and in a doze was deeply calmed in the daydream. The music fluted off while her image faded and was replaced by one called up, of a sailboat becalmed on a sea glassy as a mirror, the current halted dead and not a whiff in the air to dry their sweat. He and several mixed crew sprawled in the stern. It was too stuffy to go below. Through the days they drowsed, smoking, buying beer from the skipper or just chugging water, wondering when the wind would freshen. They ate tepid sandwiches. The skipper said there was no fuel for the engine---- drums were lashed on the deck empty. They all joked about getting out the oars. Anxiety was thick but enervating, the barometer stuck in place. The radio could not be played for music, to save the batteries. It was a piano he heard in his head then, not a harpsichord. There was no 'dialogue of wind and wave', nor was their conversation lively either. The skipper puttered around the foredeck, and no one knew who was supposed to be on watch. But there was little to watch for. It was cool and witching in moonless nights. Peering over the side he saw a galaxy of lucent streaks fomented by shoals of darting fish. Shapes larger swept by like jolly ghosts. A hand dragged in the water glowed with pearl fire. Dazzling against a vast and perfect blackboard sky irrevocable stars bristled. The mast pointed straight up with hardly a nod. No one broke out of trance. Not until afternoon of the third day was there enough breeze to luff into Cabo. He left the 'cruise' there, took a bus to La Paz and slept in a hotel before flying back. It had been a true 'lark' in four days. These images faded too, revealing one of an hourglass, spectral in the roof plaits. The music was gone. He realized the sun had gone as well, once more behind the mountain, and so had Tao. He was awake now to his last afternoon. The sand in the top of the hourglass was close to gone, and he imagined the residue sifting below.

34

THE SHOWER JOLTED HIM sensible instantly; the water was nearly as cold as the creek. One day he'd put in a heater. He stood dripping outside the bathroom where, jammed into a chicken wire lattice, a shard of mirror reflected only by zones the face he was shaving. It looked pale from the chill, dolorous from the scraping. Moving back a bit, he considered how hard it was to read your own face! You could *make* faces at yourself in hope of tricking it into revealing something, but would you know if it did? It was easy to spot vanity, perhaps even to descry temperament and appetite, but it was only another who might see through the window of the eyes into 'the soul'. To themselves, the eyes in the mirror gave back nothing more than abstruse consolation, a mystery visual and emphatic. And when those elusive eyes looked away, the world became the 'mirror' for other mysteries too lovely to demand understanding, so reading the face was easily forsworn----as though sacrificed on a more salient altar.

After grabbing on clothes and lighting the lamps, he set the bottle of raicilla on the table. Better than three quarters gone, enough was left for the one last night---and its lightened load of sand. The parota sheltered the house from daylight, but it roiled

outside in the bay, and on the hill across it the scrub fumed in a
yellowish glow beneath thirsty palms. The used pots and dishes
were scraped, cleaned and put away for next time, and sheepishly
he thought of the richer fare awaiting him in California.

He heard Becky hallooing from the path, and then she was on
the stoop in a fancy skirt and long shirt, with a tight coral necklace
spiking her throat. Silver bracelets chimed on both wrists as she
swept into the house and floated down in a chair. Her cheer was
like a confection, and he leaned over to lick her with an eager
kiss. She acted as if she was surprised, but with an air of drama
told him how well her work was going and, almost in the same
breath, that she *would* be going back to Belgium soon. The family
matter had calmed down, but getting back a little early would be
good. She needed better canvas and paint to do what she wanted.
He was astounded by her ease, and chided himself for his earlier
anxiety. Looking into her eyes, serpent green in the lamplight----
another chameleon mystery----his introspection at the shaving
mirror seemed ridiculous. If her eyes were a window to her soul,
the shades were down, so it was only her body he was reading. The
script was tantalizing, and he watched her movements and heard
the timbre of her voice smitten by their piquancy.

It was she who poured the raicilla, gulping it down without
salt or limon and pouring a second before he'd even lifted his
glass. She was telling him about the girl who came to sweep her
house, one of Ramon's daughters, and how she had wanted to try
making a drawing. "The girl has some talent, but what a dreamer
with a broom!" Maybe the two traits went together.

She got up abruptly, danced to the kitchen and commented on
how neat it was. "Let's go to the Yacht Club," she sang, dancing
back to stand in front of him with a deliberate grin, "before we
don't want to go!" He let this pass, liking the grin, but thinking of
no raunchy riposte. Was he up to it? No doubt, though making
love three or four times in a week was more than he recalled
Moses prescribing.

Pocketing flashlights, they went out into the garden but hesitated in the gloaming feathered under the moonless canopy of the parota to admire it. Laundry flapped on a line in the breeze, a scarecrow shirt for tomorrow's trip. The plants crept voiceless along the haphazard brick pathway, respiring the cool air in what seemed animal-like relief. Through Octavio's little gate and down to the gully, where the datura bells flourished agape with immodest invitation. Becky plucked a blossom, making a mock sad face, and called it her souvenir as she shoved it stem first in a shirt pocket so it resembled a badge. She continued to bounce down the trail ahead of him, and they reached the village panting in front of Eva's ramada. Eva sat in her usual spot, stockings rolled to her shins, and chuckled her familiar ditty, but shot him a private wink as if in approval. A large tank of propane fed a blazing filament light. A few cronies were sitting with her, drinking beer.

They went down the cobbled way past the tiendas to the front of Juan Cruz's compound. The patriarch himself was sitting under the portal in a chair tilted sharply against the wall, seemingly comprehending the whole of earthly life, while his family busily conducted business around him. Glaring lights surrounded the scene: Juan had a generator. His gold-toothed smile beamed expansive, his greeting hearty, giving decisive assurance that all was well tonight. He went up and spoke a few pleasantries to his venerable landlord while, for the first, Becky hovered on the path, a bit awkwardly, though Juan was her landlord too. A horse was being unsaddled nearby, neighing with obvious pleasure. Juan's wife, Clementina, could be seen inside the store, lamplight blinking off her glasses, wrapping something in brown paper. She it was who wrote him a receipt every January for the year's rent--- less than a month had cost for his last city apartment.

They went down the ramp to the village beach, where they stopped, lounging against a large canoa hauled up for the night, to take in the scene beside the quiet drain of river. Activity of commerce was scarce now, but some villagers stood around chatting. Children scurried in the sand, collecting unwary hermit crabs; a favorite pastime of his son as well. The colors of evening shone saturated in slicks stranded by the ebb tide. An air of excitement dithered there at the navel of the village, shivering in minute electric whorls, enabling the effortless attention to making do with what was at hand.

A small crowd could be seen in the Yacht Club, which was just a bare cement platform roofed over with palm fronds and panels of corrugated plastic. Boisterous voices caromed; overriding the sound of relaxed waves, a boom box blasted current rancheros. The Lucinda and a dozen pangas rolled at anchor. On the rock wall outside the restaurant some older boys sat sniggering, eyeing the girls and savoring impatiently their futures.

Suddenly, a rocket fizzed up into the sky from the far beach and burst with an uncanny retort into the familiar starry flecks, illuminating the whole bay for seconds happily drawn out. There were shouts and screams all around, and people smashed over thresholds to look. Howard was at his stunts again. He, a stumbling drunk on the beach some days, turned himself into a 'master of fire' some nights, practicing a sort of transmutation by shock, and in these moments he was a 'blood brother' to the smiths and potters whose crafts were sold in his wife Rita's tourist shop. Becky had bent down to pick up something in the sand, and jumped with fright at the noise, but then shouted happily in seeing the streamers of colored fire. The vastness of night shrank diminutive in the dying glow, and when it was all gone out it was missed, leaving hope for another. Often, Howard obliged, but the wait was in vain this time. He leaned against the canoa and watched himself watch. The unexpected could be counted on to release the unsuspected, and in the intrusive glare of the simple rocket he had gotten a glimpse of himself that did not dissipate with the sparkle, but lingered disquietly even in this rowdy ambience. It was not seeing yourself as others saw you but as the gods saw you. Invented 'reality' had to be outstared even if Time couldn't be, because that reality was essentially ambiguous with its façade of fragile cloth that splayed sheer in the power of cognizance. There was no way to know who or what the gods were, but it was evident *why* they were: for structures of existence, metaphors of mind, instigators of feeling and emotion seemingly ingenerate. No matter whether from religion, science or poetry, what is called the order of Nature is nothing if not configured by the grace---or whim---of the gods. Though they reveal themselves grudgingly---and then only to those who coax them---the gods are far from indifferent, for they have more of a stake in our existence than we have in theirs, as if they entrusted their destiny to us. Beseech them, for they are spoiled by their triumphs but protecting of their failures. Yet we might hear in the clack of palm fronds, the crash of waves or the cry of a bird, an answer to our suppliance.

Gods of grace and mischief, of felicity and doom---of sea and sky, rock and tree---inviting but uninvited. A god had ridden up with the rocket, and when the flecks of it failed, and the sparks of it faded, the god seemed to hold on by the real stars, grinning. *His* gods were a beardless grinning sort, lips pursed for a whistle. They did not growl or grunt; that was appropriate to Man, still half beast. And he, one of these beasts, was arched in the night against the satisfying bulk of the canoa, watching himself watch unspent by rumination, and trusting he could slide through an hour or two of amiable social exchange 'in the midst'; though he was in a fever, it was not a dire syndrome. The woman next to him was still exclaiming over the spectacle while he was swearing to himself he would not forget a single second of the last minute's magic, but he knew it was a vow compromised by wishfulness. It was no easier to forge a myth than it was to turn lead into gold.

He pushed off from the canoa, grasping Becky's hand at the same time, and lunged with her across the river's trickle to the steps of the Yacht Club. Village lights now reflected off the fragmenting smoke trail drifting in the air. The trace was tenuous compared to the brazen shock at its origin, but as a metaphor it was not frail but stark.

A dozen diners or drinkers laughed and rocked in the restaurant, and they took a table near the stone wall where the local boys tussled. He did not see anyone inside he recognized, but it was early. In the kitchen---a cavern nestled against a boulder impediment that formed the back wall of the place---Angelina and her helpers were busy at the hearth. He could smell split chickens grilling, and fish. They ordered, and were silent in contemplation as they waited for their beers. With so much to be said, nothing was said. Becky's mood had slipped, plain to see, and she was fidgeting, building fury. The effect of the rocket's alchemy had not lasted long for her, neither for the few early dancers who were twisting with youthful exuberance to a disco beat, a music that seemed to be forever going somewhere it never reached. But the couples might get there somehow just in the dancing. Elusive as the outcome might be, he would get there too, in spite of the music.

They drank the beers and ate their food, indifferently. A fog of wistfulness shrouded him as he thought of his morning departure, and his eyes on their own sought images to keep secure for the weeks he would be gone. The bay just beyond the lighted shapes in the room was opaque, but he had a vision of a night after the acid trip at the hotel years ago. He and Donna with their two new friends joined a group of guests for an excursion. After dinner they were paddled across the bay in a canoe to this beach, and were then led up through the village to a Saturday *baile* in a hillside palapa cantina. So there he was on the tropical 'island' of his adolescent dreams, but it was nothing like the one he'd read of in Gauguin's journal. Dark faces surrounded the periphery, and children with huge, gleaming eyes watched as a dozen couples gravely shuffled to the polka-like strains of a native band on an old jukebox. The sound was primitive and had seemed something like an idiot Chopin mazurka played in shivaree at the time. That first visit to the village, the full strangeness of it, left as indelible an impression as the acid night itself had. The recurring creak of the oars emphatic in the bay, the trek through the dark village and the remote gravity of the faces, ensnared his credulity, or incredulity---he could never tell the difference. None of those faces betrayed any either, whichever it was, and some of them he'd get to know well in the coming years.

Becky broke the silence. Coming from her fidget, she began to flail her arms and sputter a stream of words he at first did not believe, but soon realized that she felt an urge to act regretful and hurt over their 'lark'. It was perverse: to chastise herself she proceeded to chastise him. She finished the harangue by dancing out of her chair and waving a dismissal: "I'll be gone when you come back. Have a good summer." Sweeping down the steps to the beach she turned to shout a mirthful goodbye, laughing as if to mitigate any disappointment---hers or his. The raucous throng around him took no notice. He ignored the impulse to run after, knowing it useless, and let his shoulders lift in a relinquishing shrug.

35

HE SAT FOR A time with another beer, thought of asking a girl he'd talked to briefly on the beach for a dance, but preferred to wallow in conjectures not exactly rueful. He brought them along when he left, taking his time in the stroll home. It seemed for a minute that his eyes were choked with tears that would not shed, but that was just an irksome feeling hinged on a mood more maudlin than indigo. He picked up where Becky left off: sure, there was no shortage of fault to find.

The shops were all shuttered, and the village would have been quiet if not for the barrage from the Yacht Club. But the din grew muffled as he went farther. In a house on the way, a lamp burned on a small table where people sat chatting before bedtime. When he reached the gully, the datura blossoms were jostling in the breeze; staring askant, they seemed reproachful. What would Becky do with the 'souvenir' she had stuck in her shirt pocket? Put it in the glass with the other, still stubborn with life the last night he'd been there? She had acted like a jilted girl, but was far from being one. He was actually the jilted one, though neither of them had any thought of promise, let alone of sealing one. She gave herself as freely as he had. Though his freedom had many times before been compromised willingly, at no time was it without alloy. True, just as suspicion haunted the guilty mind, so shackles bound the uncommitted. If it was dangerous for the free spirit to insist too much--- *Want not, waste not*---feeling compelled to placate another was "rich in flattering delusions"--- who said that?---and led to inevitable loss as sure as gain---another deranging paradox. Loss of wind, loss of way, loss of stillness---- loss of power. But he had to laugh, and concede how complacent such lofty thoughts could be: hadn't *he* often steered to 'any port in a storm', not hesitating to throw over the sails as if they were mere ballast?

At Rasa's gate, he saw lights in the house. He did not want to talk, but went in for a moment to say goodbye. She was pouring coffee as usual, but put it down to give him a hug. Coming and going was what happened here and was acceded to without tiresome ceremony. Everyone was transient one way or another, yet he read in her smile the promise that she would be here when he returned.

At his table he turned up the lamp. There were still fingers of raicilla in the bottle, and the two empty glasses rested with the crushed limones like an emblematic still life. He poured into one and downed it quickly, spoiling the picture but kindling his chemistry. As he downed another, almost the last, the wind smartly rose as if to fill the sails he'd *not* thrown over, and he felt stirred by its conjure of forward motion.

The sand in the imagined hourglass was running out, unlike the measureless measure of the beach sand, in a single grain of which Blake had seen a whole world..... A sand clock very different from his grammar school clock. How fitting was that name! Grammar! The grammar of language, and the grammar of behavior-----D for deportment! Obey the big rules, presided over by the tick and the tock, and he in the dock, prisoner, defendant--- uninitiated--- in short, a pupil. The measurement of time might be worth it---to tally the sentence. It was the sentence of his life, but not only his. He would sit, bored but taut on the bolted down

bench, and wonder at the oddness of being alive there in that
Now, sequestered side by side with his schoolmates, so very like
the fearful children he had imagined coming through the fields
with Becky in Flemish lands. "You", Mrs. Graylady pointed, "you
with the root beer eyes, why don't you pay attention to what I'm
saying?" barked his teacher in seventh grade, after he had given
an unseemly giggle at her history question. Despite flushing,
a singular strength filled his frame as he thought through her
question to its outer side, where the bell rang and the clock lost
its tick-tock and he could run outside into the spring sunshine
where his behavior would not have a name, loosened and let go.
At least until mother scold came later, to test how much he had
learned of the grammar of behavior. "What did you learn in
school today?" was always the first question, but hardly the last.
To Mrs. Graylady all he had said was "I don't know", and he
gave much the same answer to his mother. It was really the only
answer you could give to the grown-ups, he'd thought back then,
to the people who needed to believe they were commanders.

And now, here was a more serious clock, over which he had
only a bit more sway----the imagined clock of sand, *his* souvenir.
He tried to make out the illusive image he'd seen before in the
roof plaits, but from this angle it did not show. In the bottom
of the metaphoric hourglass were the sumptuous grains that he
owned forever now; in the top, those remaining were the paltry
few he was owed. And the bottle of raicilla had been a kind of
clock too, and he drained the last inch---the last hour--- right
from the bottle, glib with the grin of his cactus god.

36

CHOIRS OF JUNGLE SOUNDS long and well rehearsed, as though
from tiers of performers, woke him to a stalwart day blowing
harder than usual. The voices fought through the bluster, and he
knew some were of courting, some were of combat. There were
solitary singers, cries of triumph or defeat; some had voice given
only by the gusts. All were the sounds of meshing destinies, each
occurring on its own; it was a level of life that could do no more
than follow the gods unknowing.

It was as if the curtain rose in a theater, where despite the
hushing audience burst a cough---*his*---and the drama was spoiled
for the moment. He'd been tossing on the bamboo bed and found
himself uncovered, one arm flung over, fingers nearly touching the
floor; he felt the blood pulsing in their tips. The hill across the
bay emerged from gloom, and the waves battered a rival music to
the chorus. When he sat up, he could see whitecaps in the murky
bay. Branches of the parota scraped the roof in the unflagging
cadences of wind, but it was too late to do anything---Octavio
had not appeared after all---for when the light came it would also
bring an urgent panga, and he would hurry to board it. He swung

out of bed groggy and reluctant; afraid of oversleeping, he knew
he was reclaimed by the common clock.

With scant time left he made a single cup of coffee, drinking it
as he cleaned and stowed the little Turkish pot under the counter.
It was cherished as the fond talisman of an innocent alchemy
and he reflected that in some weeks he would come back to
use it again. Becky would be gone, which was fine because he
would come with 'family'. This would not be a 'lark' but the
tidy course of life. Surprised by this thought, he realized that
'larks' were what he sought most---the whole week had been one,
deliberately so. The exhilaration of raw experience, a 'lark' was
living unconsidered and without a wristwatch. On such a device
time pretended no end; the hourglass was its proper, cautionary
measure. "The seeping sand is better than the creeping hand", he
cried out, as pleased with himself as a boy with an extra cookie.
Contemplation of a watch should hinder all protest, and this idea
led him to think of Job. Why should so bad a fate fall to so good
a man? That complaint of Job ---whether or not ingenuous or
presumptuous---seemed little different than the desperate cry of
a gazelle felled by a leopard, or the furious if soundless descent
of a dying star into a black hole. So Job did not know of Satan's
challenge to God, did not know he was a pawn in their game.
Take it as a moral dilemma invented by an aggrieved soul---as if
imposed on himself---and others---that afflicted, or enlightened,
nothing else in the world. The Book of Job was a fable of the
purely human desire to outwit the regime of Nature, to "reason
with God" for repeal of a principal law: *every god is matched by
a demon.* Satisfaction in so bald a scheme, he thought, was not
perverse no matter how deeply its wisdom has been concealed---
even from those who are sure it is there.

Whether he was animist, pantheist, or simply myth-dazed he
did not know or care, but the forbidding and testy Hebrew God,
pride of his ancestors--- whose very name shalt not ever be spoken---
neither grins nor winks: so dour a god could not be his.

37

THE SEA WIND HAS not diminished. Wedges of clouds tear up in torment not far above, as if fearing to rain. As he sits in Santos' now unused canoa, dry-docked above the beach, he wonders how the panga will land. He is out of sweet time, hourglass time, waiting in cool shadow though the sun is shining fitful on the day. It will not clear the ridge for a while yet. The Earth's wobble is the wobble of the sky clock too, and by the time he comes back the sun will rise from the river, early.

He hears the buzz of a panga as it rounds the Point, and steps out to the shore, ready to go yet not ready to leave. Heavy swells roll in to his shins and he studies the boat idling back and forth as Seferino waits to bring it in closer. He will have to be quick and spry to avoid a real soak. With his sandals stuffed in the shoulder bag, his legs feel the stunning chill of the brine, his toes the swift escape of sand. The panga edges in slow and the bow is pounding up and down as his hands reach for it and he tosses in the bags, hoists himself up and swings over the side a second before the next wave. Thrown down by the suddenly reversed motor, he stumbles up to join Corinne, who is sitting forward in a brown cotton huipil, smilingly collected, ready to take care of business.

As Sef spins around and roars off to the entrance, he looks back to remember his house and on the seawall Rasa has come out to wave. When they shoot past the Rock, battered by contradictive waves rinsing off its guano, the pelicans heave up in confused sunlight to find breakfast, stranding a few cormorants huddled in their feathers, deferring day for sleep. Gibbous as an egg, the moon is slung blurred in spindrift atop the excited sea, a wan remnant of his moonstruck nights. After an abrupt veer, the pocket of bay with its village, river and beach is as suddenly gone as if it had only been dreamed, and they are skimming the shore of the open Pacific. It is not pacific; the ride is in a fair wind and they grip their plank thwart to brace against the leaps and jolts as Sef works to skim the punishing breakers. Talking means shouting but he is glad not having to talk. What would he say? The tumult excuses---or complements---their separation. Shore birds hover stiff but easy, making no way over the still-shadowed rocks.

They land next to the Hotel Rosita, below the shed where sportsmen's marlin will hang for trophies in the late afternoon. Sef slides the panga up on the beach all the way, as he is going into town with Corinne. With only slight hesitation he asks her if she would have her *mozo* Beto get word to Octavio to clear his roof of the offending branches. Finding a smile she agrees and wishes him a good trip. Now with spare clock time to spend, he heads off to the courtyard of the hotel to have an indulgent breakfast, choosing a table with a view, through bending palm trunks outside, of the coast he has just sped past. The rooms of the hotel obstruct the top fronds, and he is gazing through an archway to beyond the pool, where children are splashing noisily. His gaze probes in the roll of mountains about halfway to far Cabo Corrientes---a knee poking into the Pacific---to discover the tiny indentation in the rising mist where he knows the little bay of his village is tucked away and hidden even to those who know it is there.